OBJECTS OF WORSHIP

CLAUDE LALUMIÈRE

ChiZine Publications

FIRST EDITION, THIRD PRINTING

Objects of Worship © 2009 by Claude Lalumière
Jacket illustration and design © 2009 by Erik Mohr
Spot illustrations © 2009 Rupert Bottenberg
All Rights Reserved.

LIBRARY AND ARCHIVES CANADA CATALOGUING IN PUBLICATION

Lalumière, Claude
Objects of worship / Claude Lalumière ; editors: Brett Alexander Savory & Sandra
Kasturi ; illustrator: Rupert Bottenberg ; graphic design/cover artist: Erik Mohr ;
introduction writer: James Morrow.

ISBN 978-0-9812978-0-4 (bound).--ISBN 978-0-9812978-2-8 (pbk.)

I. Savory, Brett Alexander, 1973- II. Kasturi, Sandra, 1966- III. Bottenberg,
Rupert IV. Title.

PS8623.A465O25 2009   C813'.6   C2009-903942-7

CHIZINE PUBLICATIONS
Toronto, Canada
www.chizinepub.com
info@chizinepub.com

Edited by Brett Alexander Savory
Copyedited and proofread by Sandra Kasturi

TABLE OF CONTENTS

INTRODUCTION

GODS OF DESIRE:
THE EROTIC THEOLOGY
OF CLAUDE LALUMIÈRE

BY JAMES MORROW

Surely we can all agree that the universe would be a better place if Claude Lalumière had been put in charge of its clustered suns and interstellar gases, whereas, alas, the job instead went to the anthropocentric, xenophobic, sexophobic, misogynist, bloody-minded, egomaniacal, and generally unimaginative Supreme Being of the Western religious tradition. But despite Lalumière's lamentable lack of godhead, speculative fiction aficionados have many reasons to acquire and read *Objects of Worship*. Minimalist in style, plenary in scope, elliptical in sensibility, and abrim with sardonic humour, the present collection affords its readers far more food for thought than any quantitatively equivalent swatch of Holy Writ.

Conventional wisdom holds that, while literary fiction is concerned primarily with plumbing the human psyche, genre fiction derives its appeal from narrative twists and turns. It seems to me that *Objects of Worship* occupies a third domain. These twelve stories are not so much character-driven or plot-driven as drive-driven. Lalumière's protagonists exhibit the sorts of yearnings and proclivities that our most respected social institutions teach us to mistrust: erotic energy, artistic mania, idiosyncratic mysticism, impassioned empathy with the natural world. These characters constitute a rogues gallery of sexual, political, and culinary outsiders. On page after page we profit from the appealing company of misfits, bohemians, eccentrics, visionaries, loners, losers, gays, lesbians, bisexuals, and zombies, all determined to prevail in a world that has no particular use for them.

Forces both rational and irrational contrive to keep Lalumière's oddballs and dissenters from getting what they want. Whereas the protagonists of much speculative fiction, including the characters in my own satiric epics, turn to the official epistemology of the secular West—experimental science—for insight and empowerment, we find little enthusiasm for that worldview in *Objects of Worship*. In one of those pranks so beloved by the laws of caprice, our author was born with a name that evokes the 18th-Century

Enlightenment, "le siècle des Lumières," the joke being that Claude Lalumière has cultivated a decided chariness toward that heritage and its technological stepchildren. A major character in "Hochelaga and Sons," the narrator's hapless father, was once "a disposable guinea pig" subjected to atrocious Nazi medical experiments performed in the name of science. "Roman Predator's Chimeric Odyssey" unfolds in the aftermath of a "BioWar" that sterilized much of the planet, leaving it to the descendents of "laboratory-created hybrids." "This Is the Ice Age" thrusts the reader into a frozen dystopia inadvertently wrought by "the rogue R&D department of some corporate weapons manufacturer."

If Lalumière regards the empirical with suspicion, he brings an equally wary eye to the empyrean. In the universe of *Objects of Worship*, all deities are guilty until proven innocent. The nebulous gods of the title story cheerily suck up oblations from humans and give them nothing in return but grief. The plot of "Hochelaga and Sons" turns on the Hebrew God's preoccupation with *treyf*, unclean things, a proscription that tragically prevents the hero's fantastically gifted brother from confounding a terrorist threat called the Hegemony of Hate. "The Sea, at Bari" dramatizes an encounter between a troubled young man and a nightmarish beast that can be exorcised only through a grisly variation on the eucharist. "The Darkness at the Heart of the World" and "A Visit to the Optometrist" both feature Yamesh-Lot, the kind of foul Lovecraftian lord who reminds us of the recurrent disconnect between embracing the supernatural and doing the right thing.

OBJECTS OF WORSHIP

For all Lalumière's religious skepticism, it's clear that he would sooner cast his lot with an imaginative metaphysics than with any sort of Skinnerian utopianism or Newtonian instrumentalism. Not all of the transcendent beings in *Objects of Worship* are malign. "Spiderkid" gives its readers a moving celebration of the world's arachnid deities, "all degraded memories of God . . . the primordial Spider who wove the universe into being." "The Darkness at the Heart of the World" presents the mythos of the Shifpan-Shap, avatars of a Gaia-like "Green Blue and Brown God" locked in perpetual conflict with the demonic Yamesh-Lot. In "Njàbò" we meet a sympathetic female elephant-god who refuses to forget how ruthlessly the human species arranged the extermination of her kind.

Beyond the more obvious sorts of deities, we find herein an abundance of those cape-flaunting, long-underwear-clad, quasi-divine protagonists known as superheroes. While I personally harbour a profound indifference toward this particular aspect of popular culture, I must admit that certain writers of a postmodern bent have spun their childhood affection for Superman and his descendents into beguiling works of fiction, among them Michael Bishop's *Count Geiger's Blues*, Michael Chabon's *The Amazing Adventures of Kavalier & Clay*, and Jonathan Lethem's *The Fortress of Solitude*, achievements to which we must now add three stories from the present volume, "Hochelaga and Sons," "Spiderkid," and "Destroyer of Worlds."

It's clear that Lalumière has thought through the most severe critique of the superhero ethos, namely, that the sort

10

of justice it seems to recommend partakes of vigilantism at best and fascism at worst. At his earliest convenience, around the midpoint of "Hochelaga and Sons," the author presents a taxonomy of superheroes in which the troublesome "crimefighters" are accorded the shortest entry, for his heart clearly lies with the cosmic "protectors" and the romantic "adventurers." Lalumière knows perfectly well that the promiscuous violence and casual apocalypses of Marvel Comics are, to use Susan Sontag's memorable phrase, "in complicity with the abhorrent." "But perhaps it was time for all this to end," muses the unnamed protagonist of "Destroyer of Worlds." "For another world, perhaps a better world, to be born from this one's destruction . . . Perhaps I was full of shit—justifying a monstrous offer I could not bring myself to refuse."

And so it happened that Lalumière's enthusiasm for Jack Kirby, Steve Ditko, and other such graphic storytellers ultimately won me over. Indeed, before I'd finished *Objects of Worship*, Lalumière had himself emerged in my eyes as a kind of offbeat superhero—several, in fact. In the following pages you will meet an authorial persona we might call Lord Libido, that is, Lalumière the paladin of eroticism, as well as Doctor Vegan, that is, Lalumière the crusader for animal rights, not to mention Irony Man, the Lalumière who understands the ubiquity of thwarted human intentions, plus The Eclectic Ranger, the Lalumière who has synthesized many narrative traditions into a dozen entrancing tales—tales from which I shall keep you no longer.

OBJECTS OF WORSHIP

CLAUDE LALUMIÈRE

ILLUSTRATIONS BY RUPERT BOTTENBERG

THE OBJECT OF WORSHIP

The god settles on the table. Rose tears a piece from her toast, slathers a heap of cream cheese on the ear-sized morsel, and lays it next to the god. It consumes the tribute.

Rose smiles as the god's warmth permeates her body, enfolds her heart. She squeezes Sara's hand. "Your turn."

With an irritated sigh, Sara cuts a thin—too thin, Rose thinks—sliver from a slightly unripe banana. Sara's hand moves toward the god, but Rose grabs her wrist.

"That's not enough. At least put some peanut butter on it."

Rose recoils from Sara's glare.

"I don't need you to tell me how to worship." But Sara nevertheless dips her knife into the jar and smears a dollop of chunky peanut butter on her tribute before offering it to the god.

Rose runs the six blocks from home to the video store. As assistant manager, it's her responsibility to open the shop in the morning. Rose usually gets to the store a half-hour early; she likes to attend to her morning tasks unhurriedly. But today the home god was too upset. It hates when she and Sara fight, or even when they exchange tense words. After breakfast, they had to cuddle silently on the couch with the god nestled between them until harmony was restored. When Rose and Sara finally kissed, the god rewarded them.

Rose looks at her watch as she reaches the storefront. She's made it with five minutes to spare. Two of the employees are waiting outside. And smoking. They know the staff rules. No smoking in front of the store. If they have to smoke, they should do it in the alley, or at least not so close to the door.

"We're not on the clock yet, so don't get on our case," says Vandana as she stubs out her cigarette under her black construction boots.

"Yeah," Maddie concurs, flicking away her own half-smoked cigarette with her long, crooked fingers. The green polish is flaking off her chipped, overlong nails.

Rose unlocks the front door, steps inside, then quickly punches in the security code on the pad next to the light switch. Ashley—cheerful and perfectly groomed, as always—arrives; Rose waves in all three clerks before locking the door again, so they can ready the store. But first things first.

The store god rests in its altar, which is carved into a

column next to the counter. All four women kneel, cooing prayers at the god. The god glows, acknowledging their presence, but does not otherwise stir.

By the time the store opens, they're six minutes late; only one customer is waiting. Rose apologizes, but the woman—a tall redhead with a striking face, long luxurious hair, and big curious eyes—laughs it off. "I just got here." Her smile is playful; it's enough to wipe away the remains of Rose's tension.

Rose is grateful for this change in the day's course. She should thank the store god. There's a box of chocolates in her desk. She'll bring one out for the god. Maybe mint cream? Or almond crunch?

Suddenly, the god moans painfully.

The god darkens.

Vandana, Maddie, and Ashley are already trying to soothe it by singing to it. The store god loves song, but the clerks' efforts are having no effect.

The only customer—that beautiful redhead—is browsing through the new releases as if nothing untoward was happening.

Rose walks up to her. "Have you greeted the god?"

The woman frowns and tries to suppress a chuckle. "What? . . . No."

"The altar is by the counter. Perhaps a small prayer?"

"I don't think so."

Gods must always be greeted. It's the same everywhere. Showing proper respect to the gods is what holds society together.

Rose just stares blankly at the woman, who resumes browsing. She picks a shrinkwrapped DVD case off the rack. *Burning Sky*, Rose notices, remembering that Sara had asked her to bring a copy home.

The customer walks to the counter, holding the DVD. Rose follows her.

The three clerks are still trying to soothe the god, but it is more anxious than ever. Smoke spews from the altar.

The customer turns toward Rose. "Can I buy this?"

Rose snatches the DVD away. "Please leave. Right now."

"Because of that thing," she points at the god, "you won't take my money?"

"Get out."

After the woman has gone, Rose fetches the box of chocolates from her office and, piece by piece, feeds all of it to the god. Finally, the god appears to calm down.

Then the god leaves its perch, finds the DVD the woman had intended to buy, and destroys it.

Above the bed, in its niche in the wall, the altar lies empty. Rose stiffens and stops herself from reminding Sara that it needs to be cleaned. This has been such a stressful day; Rose wants it to end on a good note. But Sara's neglect nags at her.

Sara sighs. "I'll clean it tomorrow, okay? I can tell it's bugging you."

They hug, their breasts touching under the covers. Sara continues, "You shouldn't second-guess me so much. I know your family does things differently, but I've always taken good care of the god. We live in harmony."

The god's been in Sara's family for generations. Sara had been given to her mother by the god. And the god had given Sara's mother to Sara's grandmother . . . Sara grew up with the god, has spent her entire life with it. She and the god are ritually bonded; there are duties the god won't allow anyone else to perform. But Sara is not as fastidious as Rose would like.

"You're still thinking about it." Sara, grinning mischievously, tickles Rose.

"No, stop!"

Sara pins Rose down, holding her wrists tight against the mattress. She bends toward her and almost kisses her, almost lets their lips brush.

Rose snags Sara's lower lip between her teeth, and Sara lets herself slide down on top of her lover. They kiss. Sara jams her leg between Rose's thighs. They squirm against each other. They love each other.

Noise awakens Rose. It's still dark. She groans, knowing how hard it can be for her to get back to sleep when she's roused in the middle of the night. She looks up; the altar is still empty. The god usually watches over them at night.

Sara snores, lost to sleep.

Worried, Rose gets out of bed and grabs her robe. She follows the source of the sound.

Through the kitchen window she looks at the large inner courtyard shared by five neighbouring houses. The gods are gathered. The gods are singing.

OBJECTS OF WORSHIP

A few other neighbours are sitting on their balconies, watching the gods.

All thirteen resident gods are there—one for every household with access to the courtyard. One of the gods lies in the middle of a circle formed by the other twelve. One by one, each god leaves the circle to rub itself against the god in the centre. They go around many times. With each round the singing intensifies, until it reaches a thunderous crescendo and all the gods swarm toward the centre. Abruptly the singing stops, and the mass of congregated gods pulses with light.

Rose returns to bed, troubled and confused. Before moving in with Sara, Rose had never seen gods together, and she is still unfamiliar with their social habits. Unsettled by them, even. It's a city thing, with so many households close together. Rose is still a country girl at heart, despite having lived here for three years.

Eventually, just as dawn breaks, the god returns to its altar. Rose has not slept the whole time.

Rose whispers a prayer to the god as it settles in. The god glows. Then the god joins Rose in bed, slips under the covers. It rubs itself against Rose's toes, her soles, her legs, her stomach, her breasts . . . It shares its warmth with Rose. Rose's heart melts with love for the god. The god presses itself between her legs. She spreads her legs. The god accepts the tribute of her moistness. And then the god gives itself to Rose.

Rose gasps.

Rose makes pancakes for breakfast. Lots of pancakes. With blueberries in them. She lightly sautés sliced apples and bananas, to serve on the side.

Yawning, Sara emerges from the bedroom. "Babe, it smells so delicious!"

The table is already set. Plates. Cutlery. Juice. Pot of coffee. Mugs. Can of maple syrup.

"Do I have time to shower, or should I eat now and shower after?"

"The pancakes'll keep warm in the oven."

"Fuck it. That smell is too delicious. Let's eat now." Sara sits, and Rose brings the pancakes and the sautéed fruit.

Sara asks, "What's all that ruckus outside?"

"I think one of the neighbours is moving."

"Yeah . . . Didn't Jocelyn say she might be leaving? Something about a new job?"

"Maybe. I don't know. I don't really know her."

"Ah, who cares? Let's eat this great food before it gets cold. Thanks so much for making this, babe."

Sara stuffs herself like an enthusiastic child, grinning at Rose the whole time.

The god settles on the table. Together, the two women offer it an entire pancake, with banana and apple slices on top. The god consumes the tribute. The god hums.

Sara chokes.

Rose pats her on the back, and Sara coughs, clearing her throat.

"I've never heard the god sing like that after receiving tribute. Wow. It must love your pancakes."

"Maybe." Rose can't keep the hint of something more out of her voice.

Sara looks at Rose quizzically. "What aren't you telling me?"

Biting her lower lip and keeping her eyes focused on the god, Rose says, "I'm pregnant."

Sara skips a few beats. Then, "When . . . ?"

Rose turns toward Sara. "This morning. At dawn. The god . . . it stayed out all night with the other neighbourhood gods. Singing. And something else. Dancing, maybe?"

Sara says, tersely, "They must've been saying goodbye to the god who's moving away. But whatever."

"Oh. That makes sense. Anyway, when it returned. It—"

"The god made you pregnant."

"Yes."

"You."

"Yes! I'm blessed! What will we call her?"

Sara looks away.

Rose gets up from her seat and hugs Sara. "I'm sorry, love. I'm sorry it wasn't you. I know I should've woken you, so you could be with me and pray to the god . . . but it was so sudden. So fast." She runs her fingers through Sara's hair. "Aren't you happy for me? For us?"

"Yeah . . . sure. It's just so . . . unexpected. I wasn't thinking about children at all. Not yet, at least. It's just kind of a shock. That's all."

Sara skips a few more beats, but in her silence she strokes Rose's arms.

Then, "Of course I'm happy, Rose. It's going to be great having a baby. Plus, with your looks, our daughter's gonna be cute as a button."

The god wedges itself between the two women, settling against Rose's belly, enveloping the family in a cocoon of divine warmth.

The moon is nearly full, the starry sky cloudless. The night air is a bit chilly; Rose and Sara are cuddled under a thick red quilt, pressed against each other and holding hands. They're waiting for the gods to come out.

The new neighbour moved in earlier today, but neither Rose nor Sara has seen her. After dinner, Sara told Rose that, their first night, new gods are always welcomed by the resident gods. Sometimes, new gods will vie for dominance, especially rural gods, unused to the proximity of other gods. It never unfolds quite the same way, and it can be quite a spectacle.

So here they are on the back porch. Waiting. They wave at their neighbours. Everyone is out tonight, to witness the welcoming of the new god.

Time passes, and nothing happens.

Rose asks, "Does it usually take this long?"

"No. But let's wait for it. It's worth it." Sara kisses Rose, and they neck. Waiting for the gods.

Rose is woken by Sara's snoring. Dawn is breaking. "Shit. I missed it."

Tabitha, their upstairs neighbour, yells down: "You didn't miss anything. The gods didn't come out. I'm gonna need so much coffee today." Tabitha stomps back inside and slams her back door shut.

Maddie called in sick at the last minute. Rose, unable to find a replacement, is stuck working the evening shift at the video shop. She calls home, to apologize. She's surprised that Sara doesn't pick up. She leaves a voicemail message.

It's a slow night. Petra and Ashley would have been able to handle it. The rules insist on a minimum staff of three, though, and Rose could lose her job if she left early and management found out. Ashley would probably rat her out; and she might get Rose's position if she did. It's not worth the risk, especially with a baby on the way.

At eight o'clock, while Petra and Ashley are taking a cigarette break out back, Sara walks into the store. Rose perks up. "Hey, you came by! Thanks."

Sara's carrying a little paper bag. "For you."

Rose opens it and finds an almond croissant. She leans over the counter and gives Sara a quick kiss on the lips.

Rose breaks off a tiny morsel of the croissant and hands it to Sara. "Would you . . . ?"

"Uh . . . sure." Irritation flashes on Sara's face, but she forces a grin. She places the tribute on the god's altar, hurriedly singing a line from a children's ditty. The god accepts the tribute.

"See, I even remembered to sing. Be right back."

Sara quickly scans the shelves and picks a DVD. Walking back toward Rose, she waves it in the air. "Weren't you supposed to bring one of these home?" It's a copy of *Burning Sky*.

"Shit. I forgot. Sorry. Take it, and I'll handle it."

"Alright, babe. I gotta go. I might be out late tonight. Don't wait up."

Sara gives Rose a quick peck on the cheek and is out the door before Rose even has time to utter, "What?"

Rose presses her face against the window. Already across the street, Sara walks away briskly, arms entwined with another woman's. A tall woman with long red hair.

The home altar is still filthy. The god is flaccid, discoloured. Sara has been neglecting it.

In Sara's absence, Rose offers tribute to the god, but it ignores her.

Rose worries about her baby.

When Sara finally gets home in the middle of the night and slips into bed, Rose feigns sleep.

The god instantly latches itself onto Sara, glowing brightly. Through half-closed eyelids Rose sees it take tribute from Sara's mouth, drinking her saliva.

The god darkens, oozes stinking grey goo all over Sara, all over the bed. It rushes out the bedroom.

"Oh, fuck!" Sara wipes her face on the clean underside of the pillowcase.

"You kissed her," Rose accuses. "That woman. That heathen."

"Not heathen. Atheist. Heathens worship invisible gods. Jane doesn't worship at all."

"How can anyone not worship the gods? They are with us."

"Whatever. Let's not argue." Sara gets up, walks to the bathroom, and cleans herself with a wet towel.

Rose follows her in. "I've met her before. At the store. She angered the god."

"Yeah, she told me. She was scoping out the neighbourhood. Jane's our new neighbour."

"An atheist? The resident gods won't accept her. It'll cause trouble for everyone. Look what you did to our god."

"Well, maybe we don't need the gods."

"The gods give us life, give us children."

"And why do you think the gods do that? Maybe because they need us to take care of them? Is that what you want our life to be about?"

Rose clenches her teeth. "We are the chosen of the gods. We are blessed. What can be more important?"

"Listen, babe, Jane has lots of ideas that I . . . that I agree with. Things that I've been thinking about but was too afraid to discuss with anyone, even you. Talking so freely, it made me giddy. It opened me up. We just kissed."

Rose makes an exasperated sound.

"Okay, well, maybe a little more. But it was just tonight. I was swept up by the evening. I still love you. And the baby."

"What about the god?"

"I didn't say I wanted to change our way of life . . . but things might not be how they seem, how we believe they are. Maybe society should change. It's worth thinking about, that's all."

"So . . . how does she live?"

"Well, she doesn't keep a god. Other than that, she's just like everyone else."

"But that's no life."

"Why not?"

"There's nothing to connect her to the harmony of the world. It's an empty existence. Meaningless. And it's irresponsible. Selfish."

"You don't understand. Maybe you should meet her. She's knowledgeable about the gods and their relationship to us. Talk to her."

"Never. Especially not while I'm pregnant. Promise me you'll stop seeing her. For the baby's sake."

"Rose . . . I can't do that. You can't dictate to me. Or blackmail me like that."

Both of them stay silent for a few minutes, while Sara gets fresh linen.

Rose helps Sara change the bed. "You saw how the god reacted tonight. If I can't stop you from seeing her—at least be careful. Please. But . . . I don't know what to do. About us. I don't know if I really believe that you still love me. Maybe I don't trust what you're becoming."

Sara didn't come home last night. She didn't even leave a message.

Rose is tired. It was a big day for new releases, with nonstop waves of customers. She unlocks the door to the apartment, wondering if Sara is gone for good.

Rose walks in to devastation. The couches are shredded. The television is on the floor, the screen shattered. Most of what was on the walls or on shelves is now on the floor, in pieces. The kitchen is a mess of broken china and splattered food. Everything is covered in dark, stinky slime.

The god.

Rose rushes to the bedroom. The bedroom is mostly intact, with only a trail of dark slime leading to the altar. The god rests in its niche, exuding dark smoke. The air is thick and odorous. Rose coughs.

"What the fuck . . . Rose . . . ?"

Rose turns to see Sara enter the bedroom.

"What happened here?"

"What do you think? You're so selfish. You didn't come home last night. You can't just abandon the god like that. If you want to leave, fine. Leave. But there are rituals."

"I'm not leaving. We just talked late into the night yesterday. I didn't even sleep. It was simpler to go straight to work from Jane's."

"You think I'm stupid? The god knows what's really happening."

"Maybe the god doesn't know as much as you think it does."

They don't talk for the rest of the evening. Sara cleans up the apartment while Rose tries to comfort and placate the god.

In silent agreement, both women climb into bed at the same time, their backs turned. The god slips in between them. The women turn toward the god, toward each other. The god's warmth is so delicious. Rose is surprised when Sara kisses her, and she's surprised, too, that she lets her.

The god hasn't accepted tribute of any kind for days. It rarely leaves its altar, now, which Sara still hasn't cleaned. It reeks.

Sara is snoring, but Rose wakes her up. "We need to talk."

"Can't it wait, babe? I'm too tired."

"No. It can't go on like this."

"Fuck. What are you talking about?"

"Look at the god. You're ignoring it."

"So what? Why don't you take over? I'll even help with the transfer ritual. You care about the god a lot more than I do. And clearly it cares about you more, too." Sara tips her chin toward Rose's belly.

"Is that what this is all about? You're jealous!"

"No . . . I'm sorry. I shouldn't have said that." Sara sits up and gently puts her hand on Rose's arm. "Look. I don't want to worship anymore. I started thinking about this stuff before the baby. And before I met Jane. I don't mind if you still worship, but it feels wrong for me."

"What does that mean? You can't live here if you don't worship. The god can't tolerate that. Look at it. Do you want to live like that woman? She can't even walk into a store without making trouble. Things are just going to get worse unless you stop being so selfish."

"I'm not being selfish. And neither is Jane."

Rose pushes Sara away. "Maybe you should just leave. Stop pretending."

"Have you ever thought that maybe the god is the problem, and not me?"

Through the door, Rose hears voices inside the apartment. Isn't Sara supposed to be at work?

Rose walks in. Sara is sitting on the couch. With that woman, Jane.

The god is lying at their feet, collapsing on itself. Rose rushes to it, offers it her saliva, holds it against her breasts.

"What is she doing here? What were you doing to the god?"

Jane says, "Only what should be done to all of them." Sara interrupts her with a gesture.

"Rose, baby, this is for your own good. For the good of the baby. It's safer this way."

"You monsters. You were trying to kill it."

"Baby, you don't understand."

"Leave. Don't ever come back here. I'm having the locks changed. If you ever try to come near the god again, I'll call the police. I never want to see you again."

"It's my family's god, you know."

"Not anymore. The god blessed me."

Jane says, "Rose, the gods don't care about us."

"I don't want to hear your lies. Get out! Both of you!"

Sara and Jane exchange a glance, and the two of them get up to leave. Sara turns back, looks at Rose hugging the god, and opens her mouth to speak. But Rose glares at her, and she walks out and quietly closes the door behind her.

Rose nurses the god back to health. She performs all the proper rituals. The god must let go of Sara, now. It must focus on Rose and the coming baby.

The god accepts tribute again. It lets Rose clean its altar. When Rose sleeps, it squeezes itself next to her.

Rose tries not to think of Sara anymore. That woman, Jane, has moved away. Good riddance.

Rose is three and a half months pregnant. It's her birthday today. Twenty-five years old. She gives the god extra tribute at breakfast to celebrate the occasion.

Despite the god, despite the baby growing in her body, Rose feels loneliness gnaw at her as she slips into bed.

The phone rings. "Hello?"

"Hi, babe. I just wanted to wish you happy birthday. I hope it's okay that I called. I miss you."

The god gets agitated, excited. It wraps itself around the phone, presses itself against the receiver, against Sara's voice. It glows and hums.

Rose yanks the phone cord from the wall. She's been faithful to the god. It must love her, not Sara. Not Sara.

In a flash, the god darkens. It fumes and crackles. It attacks the phone and shatters it. Dark smoke quickly spreads throughout the room. The god knocks Rose onto her back. It pushes Rose's legs open.

"No!" Rose stifles a scream.

The god squeezes itself into Rose's womb. Rose feels the god inside her, twisting and thumping. Taking back what it had given her. It pushes its way out of Rose's vagina. Blood oozes in the god's wake, flowing out of her womb and spreading onto the sheets.

Silently, Rose weeps, clutching at her belly.

The god accepts the tribute of Rose's tears and consumes them.

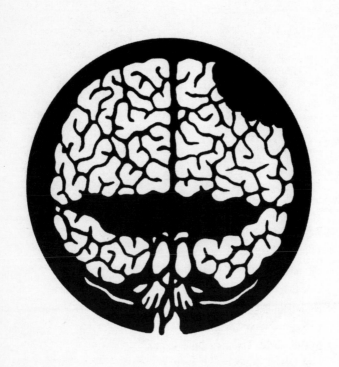

THE ETHICAL TREATMENT
OF MEAT

Raymond and George had never thought much about religion. They'd tried going to services at their local church shortly after adopting the child—it seemed like the right thing to do—but the preacher said children weren't allowed. No animals of any kind. Only people. It had never occurred to Raymond and George that there was that kind of bigotry in the world. They shopped around and found a more open-minded church about a thirty-minute drive away from their home. It was more trouble than they'd bargained for, but they wanted to be good parents.

They weren't the first ones to adopt a fleshie as a pet child—almost a family member, really—but they were the first in their neighbourhood. They decided to get a boy, hoping he'd fit in with the all-male character of their household. The agency said his name was Rod, but they didn't like that. So they called him Scott, instead. He was so cute.

They loved Scott like a son. It was biologically impossible for people to have children, and George had heard on the news that recent studies indicated that the lack of children was a probable cause of apathy and depression, an unconscious nostalgia for people's animal past. So, when George noticed that Raymond was maybe getting a little depressed, he suggested that they nip the problem in the bud and adopt a fleshie child. Even if it was expensive.

The mere idea of it had so lifted Raymond's mood that George had known it was the right thing to do. Besides, it wasn't like it was a long-term commitment or anything. Scott was already four years old; he'd only be a child for another ten years or so. Adoption was such a new fad that people didn't really know what they'd do with the fleshie children once they grew up. This was the topic of the preacher's sermon.

Scott was sitting between Raymond and George, with a gag in his mouth to keep him from shouting during the service and his hands tied to make sure he didn't remove the gag. George smiled when he noticed how affectionately Raymond kept his arm around the boy.

Most people thought that, once the children grew up, they should be sold so their brains could be used as food, or simply killed by their adoptive families, their brains eaten fresh. Fresh brains were such a rare—and delicious—

treat. That packaged stuff was never as good. Too many preservatives.

But the preacher at this church was a radical. She loudly advocated animal rights, even human rights, for fleshies. George listened. He had never considered these ideas seriously before. He used to snicker at anyone so naive as to buy into that sentimental propaganda. Glancing at the boy, he pondered the preacher's words. He wasn't convinced, but he realized that he now needed to think about all this more carefully.

Food was a problem. Pet food came in two formats. There was kibble, which wasn't too smelly, but Scott clearly wasn't that enthusiastic about it. He loved the other kind, the moist food. But neither George nor Raymond could stand the smell of the stuff, those icky vegetable, leafy, and fruity odours.

They argued about it. Raymond was willing to try, for the boy's sake. Plus, the vet said that the moist food was healthier.

George, however, was far from convinced. "No! It's just too disgusting," he said as Raymond served dinner. They were having brain casserole with chunky brain sauce. The brain cake they were going to eat for dessert was baking in the oven. It all smelled so delicious.

He continued: "And who cares if it's healthier? It's not like he's going to have a long life or anything."

Raymond looked hurt. "Don't say that! You heard what the preacher said! We have to work toward becoming a more compassionate society! To stop thinking about these animals only as a resource, a source of food. I mean, look at them, they look almost exactly like us. Sure, their skin is kind of sickly smooth, without any rot, and you can't see any of their bones or anything, but, still, they almost look like people. They can talk. They walk on two legs. It's not their fault if they smell, well, alive or something. Sure, it's kind of revolting that they grow old and then just stop moving once they die. But what we do to them in those factory farms just isn't right!"

George waited before replying. There was a tense, uncomfortable silence—save for Scott's constant crying and yelling and pounding. The boy always had so much fun when they locked him in that closet. After a few minutes, George glared at Raymond and said, "Are you done? Can I speak now?"

Raymond crossed his arms and nodded reluctantly.

"First, where do you think this meal comes from? From dead animals—animals just like Scott. This is what these animals are—food. Meat. They're our only source of food. And we have to farm them, or else we wouldn't be able to feed everyone. Do you—"

"Farming's not natural. The preacher said so! And she's right. You know she is."

George was livid. "Don't interrupt me! I let you drone on. Now you listen to me."

Pouting, Raymond said, "Okay, I'm listening."

George wagged his finger, his mouth open, ready to bark his anger at Raymond, but instead he let his arm and shoulders drop and said in a neutral voice, "Oh, what's the use." He walked out of the house.

What was really irritating George was that he found himself starting to agree with Raymond and the preacher. But he didn't want to. He hated this kind of sentimental anthropomorphizing. Meat was meat. He was starting to regret ever adopting the boy. None of this would be an issue if Raymond hadn't become so attached to Scott.

He wandered around the neighbourhood for an hour or so and then decided to go back home.

He heard the screams even before he opened the door. He walked into the living room and saw Raymond playing with the boy. Scott's screams were so loud. He must really be enjoying himself. George could see that the boy had shat and peed himself in excitement, tears and snot running down his face. Raymond and Scott looked so beautiful playing hide-the-maggots that George's anger melted away. He took a handful of maggots out of his mouth and joined the two of them at their game. Scott screamed even louder when George started pushing maggots up the boy's nose. What fun! George softened even more and gave Raymond a loving look. They kissed, the boy's screams making it all the more meaningful.

Basil and Judith Fesper were moonbathing on their front lawn when George stepped out of the house to wash the car. They waved at him to come over. Inwardly, he groaned. What were they going to complain about now? What had Scott done this time?

"Hello, Basil. Judith."

They were both smiling. Basil said, "I wanted to apologize for almost eating your boy last month."

That surprised George. "Huh . . . thanks." Scott had run away a few weeks ago, and George had found Basil Fesper about to pop the boy's skull open for a quick snack. But George had intervened just in time. Basil had said, "If I ever find that animal on my property again he'll be a meal!" Since then, Raymond and George usually kept the boy chained up to keep him out of trouble.

Judith shook her husband's shoulder. "Ask him, Basil. Ask him."

Basil looked irritated for a second, but then recovered. "What the wife and I mean is that hearing all those screams coming from your house . . . Well, it makes us yearn for the pitter-patter of little feet, you know? We're thinking about getting a little one of our own. We were wondering if you could give us the number of the agency where you got Scooter."

"Scott."

"Right. Scott. So, what's the number?"

The preacher led George through the church. George looked at the frescos depicting the seven-day meteor shower that, according to Scripture, released God's chosen from the ground and allowed them to inherit the Earth from the fleshie animals who had ruled it in prehistoric times. It was so hard for George to remember that chaotic age, centuries ago, when people first walked the Earth. All he could recall was an all-consuming hunger for fleshie brains. Scripture said the feeding frenzy before God gave people consciousness lasted another seven days, but who really knew? George had never really cared about religious dogma. He didn't see the point in arguing over details nobody could prove or disprove. Maybe people had simply been too hungry to think straight.

They reached her office in the back. She offered him a glass of brain juice. "It's organic," she said. "From free-range fleshies."

It tastes the same as regular brain juice, he thought.

Sitting behind her big desk, she asked, "Is everything alright with your family, George? How's Raymond? And little Scott?"

"Well, there's nothing wrong per se, but that is kind of why I'm here." George looked at the floor and shuffled his feet, not sure how to continue. The preacher waited patiently.

George plunged ahead. "I've been thinking a lot about all that animal rights stuff of yours. At first I was pretty dismissive of it, but now I'm not so sure. I think I might be starting to agree with you. Especially the part about how it's unnatural for people to live apart from animals. I mean, since we've adopted Scott, Raymond's happier than he's ever been. And even I have to admit that the boy's fleshie screams are soothing for the soul. They make me feel . . . I dunno . . . complete or wholesome or something. And even the neighbours, who were antagonistic when we first got Scott, have been adopting fleshie children, too." George was getting wrapped up in what he was saying, talking more rapidly. "For example, just next door, the Fespers have adopted three children. Three!" He shook his hand to emphasize his point, and a morsel of flesh snapped off his index finger and fell to the floor.

"Now, there's a real sense of community in the neighbourhood. There never was before. People throw parties and invite the neighbours to meet their new children. That kind of thing. There's never a moment without at least some screaming on our street. And it feels so right, so natural."

"I'm very glad to hear that, George. But I don't understand what your problem is."

"Well . . . I've been thinking about the appalling conditions in the factory farms, and all that. And . . . And I think I want to do more. I want to help change things. Make this a better world for others like Scott, for the fleshies."

The preacher stayed silent, scrutinizing George.

He fidgeted in his chair. "Did I say something wrong?"

"No. Absolutely not. Have you gone crazy?"

George couldn't understand why Raymond was so upset.

"You're going to get arrested. And where would that leave poor little Scott, with you in jail and only me to look after him?"

"But, Raymond, I'm doing this for Scott, so that he can grow up in a better world. I thought you'd be proud of me. That you'd want to do this, too. You're always talking about this fleshie rights stuff. Arguing with me to see things your way. And now I do. I really do. And I want to do something about it. Talk isn't enough. It won't change the world without action to back it up."

"That doesn't mean that I condone this kind of . . . of terrorism. It's criminal, George. Plus, your first responsibility should be to your family. To me and little Scott."

George was getting angry and impatient. First, Raymond fought with him because George didn't believe in animal rights, and now they were arguing because, more than simply spouting slogans, George actually wanted to do something to help the fleshies. Before he could stop himself, he yelled at Raymond, "You're such a hypocrite. Such a coward. You don't really want what's best for Scott, just what's best for yourself!" And, with that, he stomped outside and drove away, to the rendezvous point the preacher had given him.

The preacher said that they were going to hit a fleshie factory farm. Blow up walls and liberate the fleshies. Make the authorities notice that people really cared about this, that it wasn't just empty rhetoric.

There were nine of them altogether. George recognized some of them from church. They split up in three vans. One of the vans, not the one George was in, was loaded with explosives. They were going to aim that van at the wall of the farm. The explosion should blow a hole big enough to let the fleshies escape. In the confusion, they'd slip in and make sure all the fleshies were freed. There shouldn't be too many people at the plant. They'd chosen a religious holiday for their operation: the first day of the Week of the Sacred Meteors.

Well, that was the plan.

The first part went off well. They drove far out of town, to where the factory was. The driverless van hit the wall. It exploded. It brought the wall down. They waited a few minutes, but no fleshies ran out. In fact, no-one ran out.

Confused, the group advanced toward the factory. They walked through the damaged wall and into the building. Inside, they saw that the van had hit the security guard's office. His head had been torn off his body. It lay on the floor in the doorway to the corridor.

As the animal liberators walked by, the head said, "Hey! Who are you guys? What the flesh is going on here?"

The group ignored the security guard. George thought, *I sure hope that guy has good medical coverage. Recapitation's not cheap.* Then one of the guys kicked the head. The preacher got mad: "Ralph! There was no need for that!"

Ralph, who was so tall he had to bend down to walk through the doorway, looked sheepish. "Sorry. Got too revved up."

The factory felt empty, deserted. The corridor led to a number of closed doors. The preacher said, "The fleshies must be behind those doors. Come on. Let's do what we came here for."

The first door led to a broom closet. George opened the second door. Jackpot.

The room was huge. Naked fleshies were stacked in a big cage, pressed tightly against each other. Their arms and legs had been amputated, but they were still alive. There must have been hundreds of them. They were all covered in excrement. Their mouths were sewn onto transparent plastic tubes that led to a big vat above their cage. Some kind of liquid goop flowed from the machines and into the mouths of the fleshies.

George could never have even imagined these conditions.

Between the door and the cage, there was a long stretch of tables, on which were piled mountains of amputated fleshie corpses with their skulls sawn open. On the floor, there was a long and deep tub filled to the rim with unprocessed brains.

The smell of the raw brains was overpowering.

The group of animal liberators, George included, mobbed the big tub and started chomping away at the cornucopia of raw meat.

In less than an hour, the tub was licked dry. High on food, the activists approached the cage that held the live amputated fleshies. They tore the iron bars apart with their bare hands. They ripped the tubes from the fleshies' mouths. They cracked the skulls of the animals on the floor and gorged themselves on fresh brains.

They fed until they'd eaten all the meat stored at that factory.

George lay on the floor in a stupor, his body covered in

blood, gore, and brain goo. He was roused by the police sirens. Around him, the other liberators were slowly starting to come out of their post-binge daze. George, alarmed by the sound, collected himself and hurried outside. A half-dozen police vehicles were on the road, driving fast toward the factory farm. He ran to a ditch and jumped in. He prayed that the police hadn't seen him.

From the ditch, George saw the police round up all of his cohorts and search the would-be liberators' two remaining vans. After a while, they drove off. He'd managed to escape. Raymond had been right. This had been a crazy idea.

They hadn't done any good for the fleshies. All they'd done was eat.

George got angry at the preacher for putting all these stupid ideas into his head. Eating was natural. Meat was meat was meat. And that's all there was to it.

George and Raymond invited the whole neighbourhood to their backyard barbecue. The Fespers were the first to arrive, but soon dozens of people were milling about the yard, their children tied up and well-behaved, screaming and crying. Scott was tied to the fence, next to the barbecue.

Basil Fesper said, "I've never trusted preachers. All that holiness. It warps the mind."

Raymond said, "Basil, it was only that one preacher who was criminally insane. Not all of them!"

Basil harrumphed. "They're all trying to contaminate us with their subversive notions, I tell you. I'll breathe before you ever see me in a church!"

His wife giggled. "Oh, Basil! Like you need an excuse for not going to church! Honestly, if I hadn't insisted on a traditional wedding . . ."

Holding hands, George and Raymond left the couple to bicker with each other.

Raymond turned to George and said, "Darling, I don't know why I got so depressed before we got Scott, but, almost losing you because of that stupid stunt, it really put things in perspective. I love you, and that's all that really matters."

"I love you, too, Raymond. I'm sorry we fought so much. That I got so tense and angry all the time."

"And all that over an animal! Over a ridiculous fad! What were we thinking?" They laughed.

Raymond clapped his hands to get the guests' attention. "Okay everyone, I guess we should get started!"

George fired up the barbecue grill.

Everyone grabbed their children. Raymond looked at George, "He's all yours, darling."

George dug his fingers into Scott's skull and cracked it open. He was looking forward to better and better times with Raymond now that they'd worked things out. *But*, George thought, *I'll miss the screams.*

HOCHELAGA AND SONS

I slide open the door to my parents' closet. I gather the clothes that hang there and move them to the bed, laying them down gently, making sure not to wrinkle them, just like my mother would have done. From the top shelf, I take down the boxes of old photographs, forgotten gifts, and useless knick-knacks and pile them on the floor at the far end of the bedroom. I empty the closet of belts, old shoes, ratty sweaters, and rarely worn neckties. Once I'm done clearing everything out, I grab the sledgehammer and start tearing the wall down.

Because I can't become intangible and walk through it. Because I can't teleport at will. Because I can't even punch holes in it with my bare fists.

Because my father is dead. Because Bernard won't do what needs to be done.

OBJECTS OF WORSHIP

"In the Second World War, I was a corporal in the Black Watch, the Royal Highland Regiment of Canada, which was part of the 5th Infantry Brigade. On the 19th of August 1942, Canadian forces spearheaded an attack at Dieppe, in hopes of establishing a beachhead in Nazi-occupied France, and my squad took part in that operation."

It was 1988, and my brother and I were eight years old. By that point, we'd been bugging Dad for this story for as long as I could remember. He'd always put it off; he'd say, "I'm not ready to talk about that yet," but even then we knew he meant, *When you're a bit older*. Finally, he'd given in, and he knew we didn't want a kiddie version. He respected that, so he told it to us as if we were adults.

"The invasion was a disaster. War is always brutal, but this was a massacre. The Nazi soldiers slaughtered us. They started shooting at us even before we landed, and on the ground they just kept mowing us down."

Dad was sitting at the foot of our bed, telling the story with his hands as much as with his voice. Bernard and I hung on his every word. Our father's face was grim, shrouded with sorrow; his fists were clenched, subtly shaking.

"As we stormed the beach at Dieppe, artillery shells exploded around us and machine-gun fire tore into us. All the men in my squad were killed; friends of mine died that day, next to me, in front of me, all around me. But I was only wounded, unwittingly left for dead in the chaos as our forces retreated after losing thousands of soldiers."

Mimicking a wounded, unconscious soldier, Dad sprawled himself on the bed; I remember his elbow digging into my shin. Dad was never one to linger on tragedy; Dad was all about fighting against tragedy, refusing to let it win, and laughing in its face. Despite his promise to tell us the story seriously, he couldn't help hamming it up. Already, we were so wrapped up in his narrative that we didn't mind, or even really notice. It's not that he was treating us like kids, it's more that he was being genuinely himself: goofy, fun-loving, and larger than life. Even while recounting something this gruesome. Especially while recounting something this gruesome.

Dad stayed silent, eyes closed. Bernard and I exchanged wide-eyed, worried glances, completely hooked not only by the story but also by Dad's theatrics. I couldn't bear it anymore. I shook Dad's shoulder, "What happened? What happened after that?"

"The Germans must have seen that I was still alive. They captured me, but they didn't take me to a prisoner-of-war camp."

Dad sat up.

"No . . . they had other plans for me. Or, in any case, they needed a body, and mine was convenient. They took me to a laboratory in the dungeon of an old castle. I never figured out where I was exactly because I couldn't speak German then—"

"But you can speak German now, right?" I asked.

"Yes, Gordon, I can."

Bernard jumped in. "And French?"

"Yes, but so can you two. You even go to French school!"

My brother and I started listing every language we

could think of. "Spanish! Greek! Italian! Japanese! Chinese! Swahili! African! Cree! Swedish! Ontarian!"

"Some of those aren't really languages, boys."

Bernard asked, "Are there any languages you can't speak?"

"I don't think so," Dad said as Mom walked into the room. She sat behind him and hugged him, pressing herself against his back, smiling at me and Bernard.

Wrapping his fingers around Mom's, Dad said, "Now do you want to hear the rest of this story or not? 'Cause it's gonna be lights-out pretty soon."

Mom said, "Actually, it's lights-out now. The boys are so excited it'll take them hours to get to sleep as it is."

"Mom!" Bernard and I shouted together.

"Okay, okay," Dad said. "I'll jump to the ending."

Mom nodded, grinning. She slipped past Dad and squeezed between the two of us. We snuggled on either side of her, and the three of us listened to the conclusion of Dad's war tale.

"For more than two years, I was a lab rat for a team of Nazi scientists. Their research was equal parts science, torture, and occultism. They subjected me to all kinds of gruesome experiments; operated on me without anaesthetic; performed bloody rituals using my body as the focal point; irradiated me with radioactive rays; injected me with serums; forced me to drink foul-tasting concoctions that burned my throat . . . I think I even remember, at various times, having my limbs amputated, my tongue cut out, my eyes torn out . . . I have this memory of one of them reaching into my chest and ripping out my heart, holding it up above my face while its blood dripped onto my chapped lips . . . But I don't know if any of that's true. I'm not sure at all what really went on while I was their captive. Even while it was all happening, I had difficulty distinguishing fact from delirium."

Bernard interrupted. "Did they do all that to you because you're Jewish?"

"I don't know. I really don't."

Impatient, I prompted Dad to continue.

"One day, a particularly messy, gory, and complex rite was disrupted by the castle shaking. The Nazi guards ran down into the dungeon to evacuate the scientists. I recognized the sounds of an air raid: the castle was being bombed. Part of the ceiling fell, and the scientists' machines—these were like no other machines I've ever seen; I never did find out what they were or did, exactly— anyway . . . The machines exploded, destroying everything in sight. A powerful blast catapulted me into the air, and I lost consciousness. When I came to, I was naked—but, to my utter astonishment, otherwise completely unhurt, my body no longer showing any sign of the ravages the Nazis had inflicted on it. I'd landed in the middle of some woods with no idea where I was. So I just started walking, until I was found by some American soldiers. It turned out I was in Bavaria. They took me under guard, debriefed me, verified my identity, and eventually I was shipped back home to Montreal."

Mom beamed a proud smile at Dad. He smiled back,

and they exchanged glances that sparkled equally with complicity, triumph, and mischievousness. Then Mom giggled; pretty soon Dad was laughing, too.

"What's so funny?" Bernard asked.

Dad said, "Nothing. Just some old joke between your mom and me."

They kissed us goodnight and got up off the bed.

"Dad," Bernard said, "that was more than forty years ago. The principal at school fought in the war, and he's old. Real old. Like, he's retiring next year. You don't look anywhere near that old. Our Math teacher, Monsieur Savoie, he told us once that he was thirty-five, and you look younger than him."

Mom's face darkened. "You know about your father. And you know you can't ever even hint at it to anyone outside the four of us."

Dad said, "Honey, they know. Lay—"

"Let me handle this," she told him. Turning back toward Bernard, she said, "Well?"

"Yes, Mom."

She looked both of us in the eye. "You know you have to keep it a secret. You know that."

"Yes," we said in unison, doing our best to match Mom's seriousness.

There's dust in my nose, my mouth, my throat, my lungs. I should have worn one of those filter masks or something. But it's done, now; I've broken through to the concealed room behind the closet. The room where Dad kept his secret hidden from the world. The room with no doors and no windows that Dad included when he built this house after coming home from the war.

That's around the time the newspaper articles about Hochelaga started appearing.

I step inside the tiny room. There are three spare uniforms, all identical.

I undress, choking back tears.

I slip into the green jumpsuit. I put on the orange rubber boots. I pull the skin-tight orange hood over my head, lining up the holes with my eyes and mouth. I fasten the green helmet, making sure the chin-guard strap is tight enough, but not too tight. Finally, I pull on the thin white gloves.

I walk out of the closet wearing Dad's uniform. For six decades, Dad was Hochelaga, Montreal's own costumed superhero.

When Jacques Cartier arrived in 1535, Hochelaga was the name of the Iroquois village that stood on what was to be later named the Island of Montreal. "Arrived" being the polite term for "invaded," Dad had always reminded us sardonically.

Dad chose the name because it honoured the First People who lived here before the European invaders, and because it was neither a French nor an English name. It was important for him that his superhero name favour neither of Montreal's major languages. Dad, like most Montrealers, just wanted the Francophone and the Anglophone communities to get along. He spoke both languages fluently. In fact, courtesy of his multipurpose energy, he was fluent in every language spoken in the world today. Hochelaga was a hero for everybody.

And now, because of my selfish, useless brother, it's up to me to become the new Hochelaga.

Because somebody has to.

Summer 1992 in Montreal. The city's 350th anniversary. The year The Mighty came to town to see my father.

The Mighty. An elite group of international super-heroes. *The* elite group of international superheroes. They've been around since 1961, protecting the world from alien invasions, interdimensional demons, mad scientists, and other world-threatening dangers.

The day before The Mighty's visit, having no clue of what was to come, Bernard and I had had a rare quarrel. And, coincidentally, it had started with a discussion about The Mighty themselves.

"I think the Lion King's the coolest member; he's the most radical. And the most mysterious. Nobody knows if he's even really human," I said.

"Whatever. My favourite's Samson. Because he's Jewish, like us." This wasn't the first time Bernard had brought this up.

"You know we're not Jewish. Not really."

Dad was a secular Jew—and an atheist. He didn't do anything Jewish; no Yom Kippur, no Hanukkah, no religious or traditional stuff at all. No circumcisions for us. No Bar Mitzvahs. No Sabbath. No worrying about kosher. Either he didn't have any family left or he didn't speak to them. He was close-mouthed about that. And Mom wasn't Jewish at all; according to Jewish law that means we're not either.

Mom, as she liked to say, was half Louisiana Negro, half Canadian Cree, and all Montreal atheist. Bernard and I didn't look a thing like her. But we looked almost as much like Dad as we looked like each other. And Bernard turned out even more like Dad than I did.

"We're not *not* Jewish. I'm not ashamed, like Dad is."

"Dad's not ashamed. He just doesn't believe in that. In any religion. And neither do we."

"Being Jewish doesn't mean that you have to believe in Judaism. Besides, there's nothing wrong with believing in God."

"Whatever. I don't care about any of that, anyway."

But then Bernard took the argument somewhere new.

"Oh yeah? Well maybe you should care about this: there were no superheroes before the war. All that began after. Around the same time Dad became Hochelaga."

"So?"

"Dad gained his powers from Nazi experiments. And there's a bunch of Nazi scientists who vanished after the war. Maybe all the superheroes were created by secret Nazi science."

"That's stupid. Dad isn't a Nazi. The Mighty aren't Nazis."

"You don't understand. I'm not saying they're Nazis. I know they're heroes. I'm not denying all the good they do. But maybe the Nazis created all the superpowers—or Nazi science, anyway. On the backs of tortured and slaughtered Jews."

"Dad says the Nazis didn't kill only Jews. They nearly exterminated the Gypsies, they sterilized Blacks and mulattos, they murdered millions of Europeans of all kinds."

"Yeah, but they killed more Jews than they did anyone else. They hated the Jews most of all. And that's where Dad's powers come from."

I punched him. And it escalated. Mom came in to break us up, but neither of us would tell her why we were fighting.

The next morning, on our twelfth birthday of all days, the argument behind us, Bernard and I had just finished watching an episode of our favourite cartoon series, *Chuck Amuck*, and were waiting for *Katgirl & Canary* to come on, when there was a special news bulletin. The faceless red mask of the Internationalist—the leader of The Mighty—appeared on the TV screen. "The Mighty have come to Montreal in order to meet with Hochelaga on an urgent matter. We are waiting on the roof of City Hall. Montrealers, please spread this message to ensure that it reaches Hochelaga. Thank you for your time. Remember: help us make the world a better, more tolerant place." He repeated the message in French. Then, he stepped back and raised his famous shield in the air, showing its borderless world-map coat of arms to the camera.

We ran upstairs to Dad's study. "Dad! Dad! Dad!"

He met us on the stairs and signalled for us to calm

down. "I know," he said. "It was on the radio."

"Take us with you," we said.

"You know I can't. It's too risky. People can't know that Hochelaga has twin boys. Do you want a supervillain to come after you? Or your mom?"

"But it's The Mighty! We'll never get another chance to meet them. They're the world's greatest superheroes!" More than ever, the two of us were talking with one voice. For all his theories about Nazi science and superheroes, even Bernard wasn't immune to fannish excitement when it came to The Mighty.

Mom came up behind us. "No, they're not," she said, balancing herself on our shoulders and reaching over to kiss Dad, who bent down to meet her halfway. "What do you think they want?" she asked him.

"Hell if I know. Maybe the Hegemony of Hate is planning an attack on the city, and The Mighty need some local help. Something like that. With the anniversary celebrations, there's bound to be some trouble. Terrorism's not my specialty, but I'll do whatever I can."

Bernard was fuming mad that Dad wouldn't let us meet The Mighty. "You have to take us. I want to meet The Mighty."

I could see in Mom's eyes that she was getting angry with us, but I understood why we couldn't go, as much as I wanted to see The Mighty in person. "Bern—you know we can't go. Dad's right."

"No! I want to go! It's our birthday! We deserve it! We've been good! We've never told anyone! Ever. We've been so good." Turning toward Dad, he snarled, "Do you know how hard it is not to brag? But we don't. We never do. And you won't even do this one thing for us!"

Bernard was so angry his entire skin was turning red. Unable to contain his rage, he screamed and jumped up . . . and he just stood there in mid-air, defying gravity. "What—I can . . . ?" Then he zipped higher—his face flushed with panic—and banged his head on the ceiling, knocking himself out. Dad caught him before he could fall to the floor.

Dad murmured, "He flew . . ."

Already Bernard was groaning his way back to consciousness. He was going to be okay. Mom took Bernard from Dad and said, "I'll take care of him. Don't worry. You just go. Now! You're needed."

Dad looked frightened. He gave me a hug and, without another word, left to meet The Mighty.

Dad had just about every superpower imaginable— superstrength, superspeed, invulnerability, invisibility, shapeshifting, flight, teleportation, transmutation, telepathy, telekinesis, firebreathing—you name it, he could do it. There was only one catch. He could access—or activate, or whatever it was he did—only one power at a time. While he used his speed or his strength, for example, he wasn't invulnerable. He wasn't automatically immune from harm: for his invulnerability to work, he had to will it into function.

His power was like an energy field of some sort. Up to a

point, he could control the extent of the field, so that, for example, his clothes would also become indestructible, or invisible, or whatever. So I guess his power was energy, and he could harness that energy any way he wanted. He didn't fully understand it himself. He just used the power as best he could. If he didn't appear to age it was because, when he wasn't actively doing superhero stuff, he would use that energy to heal and repair his body. Theoretically, he could have been immortal.

Although Dad kept his natural, youthful appearance at home, when he presented Benoit Kurtz to the outside world he would shapeshift to look older. "Benoit Kurtz" was "Dad." But he had other identities, too. In 1976, Dad "retired" his real identity, the original Benjamin Kurtz, mimicking death (just another application of Dad's superpower) while his "son" was "away overseas." After the funeral, he teleported himself back home out of the grave, assuming "Benoit Kurtz" as his default identity. In 1998, as "Benoit" grew older, he invented a new "Benjamin Kurtz"—a "grown-up son from a previous marriage in Europe" who was our "older brother, named in honour of his grandfather." Dad was once again in the process of shifting from one identity to the next.

And he fooled everyone. Well, almost everyone.

Mom, a municipal librarian who knew "both" the "older" Benjamin and the "younger" Benoit and whom Hochelaga had once saved from a burning apartment building, figured out his secret in 1978. She teased him for months, dropping vague double entendres that could imply she knew Dad was

Hochelaga. It drove him crazy—he could have read her thoughts if he'd wanted to, but Dad would never invade someone's mind without just cause. He'd long ago set limits on what he would allow himself to do. On what was right, and what wasn't. Eventually he broke down and asked her out to dinner, telling himself it was just to scope out what she knew. But that night their long flirtation turned into love. They got married within the next year and had children in 1980. Us.

As kids we never showed any sign of being superhuman. Until Bernard suddenly manifested Dad's powers.

Me . . . I was always just a normal guy.

I have no idea what to do. As much as I hate to admit it, I feel silly in Dad's costume. Somehow, Dad managed to pull off wearing this gaudy outfit and maintain his dignity . . . but I don't know how. Maybe it was because he imbued everything he did with such low-key, charming wit. No matter how hard I try to emulate him, I know I can never match his confidence, his presence. I feel ridiculous and self-conscious, and not just because I don't have superpowers. I haven't even stepped outside yet.

But the Herald of Hate is out there, and someone has to stop him. He thinks he's killed Hochelaga. Maybe he has, but I'm hoping that the sight of me in Dad's costume will rattle him, allowing me to . . . to . . . What can I do?

Every day after Bernard manifested the power, for more than a year, I concentrated, tried to activate my own "latent" powers by force of will. But there was no power within me. For the first time in years, I try again.

All I accomplish with all this concentration is to get a nosebleed.

That is so pathetic. I am so pathetic. I have no power. I have no plan. I should have a plan. The Herald of Hate is going to slaughter me. But I have to try to take him down. For Dad. For Mom.

For me.

Bernard fully regained consciousness immediately after Dad left. At first, he couldn't control the energy. He became intangible and sank through the floor. He was gone for almost a full minute; Mom panicked. But then he came back up. Trying to rematerialize, he shapeshifted randomly, taking on the forms of various classmates, Dad, Mom, wild animals, even furniture. Finally, he became himself again, with the energy under control. He still had a bump on his head. I teased him that he could use the power to heal that, just like Dad always did, but he just grunted and told me to mind my own business. I felt we were about to quarrel again—the previous day's fight wasn't completely forgotten after all—so I backed off. We both sulked, while Mom looked anxious. We all sat in the living room and watched TV, none of us exchanging a word. I was too annoyed to pay attention, and I don't even remember what was on.

Less than an hour later, Dad returned. First thing he did was fuss over Bernard. I could see Dad was worried, but Bernard wouldn't talk to him at all. Mom surreptitiously shook her head at Dad, and he left my brother alone.

The four of us just sat there, tense and awkwardly silent, until I couldn't hold in my questions any longer. "Who was there? What were they like? What did they want? Did you help them?"

Dad laughed, and my mood brightened at that familiar, comforting sound. "Just give me a minute." He grabbed a beer from the fridge and plopped down on the couch. We all gathered around him, even Bernard.

"There were seven of them. The Internationalist, of course. I liked him. He's a bit too serious and intense, but we have the same kind of ideas about the world. I asked him to visit if he ever had the time so we could grab a beer, relax, and chew the fat. There was the Weird Witch. A real looker, that one. A tall, Slavic amazon." Mom chuckled, and Dad smiled back at her. "Anyway. The Lion King was there, too. And Thunderer. Marksman. Metal Man. Webmistress."

"Who did you fight?" I asked.

"We didn't fight anybody. They came to ask me to join The Mighty."

"You're going to be one of The Mighty? That's great!" I stood up, cheering, and did a little dance around the living room.

"I didn't say that, Gordon."

"What . . ."

"I thanked them for the offer, but I turned them down. I don't want to be away from you three more than I have to, and it's not like they're short on members, anyway. I like the good I do here, in Montreal. Let other heroes fight the big menaces. For me this is all about the people. That's what

Hochelaga is. A hero for the people."

Almost everyone thinks that superheroes are all the same. That's not true. I have this theory that, for the most part, they fall into three categories.

Take The Mighty, they're *protectors*. They save the world from catastrophes and invasions and terrorism, that kind of stuff. They don't try to find trouble. They react when threats occur. They're warriors, always ready to defend.

Then there are *adventurers*, like the Detective of Dreams or the Preservers. They explore outer space, ocean depths, mystical dimensions, or any kind of uncharted terrain...and seek out the unknown because they can. They investigate strange occurrences, just to gain more knowledge about the universe. They don't want to fight, but, when they uncover an unexpected danger, they deal with it.

And there are *crimefighters*. Like Doc Shadow or Blind Justice. They patrol at night. Foil armed robberies. Break up organized crime. Fight crazy supervillains. Avenge murders. That kind of thing.

There's some overlap, and it's not all cut-and-dried. Superheroes, like anybody, don't always fit into facile categories.

Dad wasn't really like any of those. Maybe he fit the crimefighter profile to some extent, but that's not what he was about.

What Dad liked to do most was find lost pets. Or talk to people who wanted to throw themselves off rooftops. Or get drunk drivers off the road before they hurt anyone. Or stop adults from beating on kids, husbands from beating on their wives. Expose slumlords and sweatshop owners. Protect the homeless. Be a shoulder to cry on for the desperately lonely in the middle of the night. Heal accident victims. Listen to crazy people so that they felt better about themselves, about being alive, about connecting with someone. I mean, sure, if he saw a mugging, he'd stop it. If some supervillains got the mistaken impression that Montreal would be an easy stomping ground, he'd teach them a lesson. If a weirdo cult tried to open a gateway to some demon dimension in the heart of downtown, he'd make sure they could never try something like that again. But that's not where his heart was. Dad had this way with people. He made them feel like they could talk to him, even in that crazy superhero getup of his. More often than not, he didn't have to throw a punch or get violent in any way. He'd just show up and defuse the situation by saying exactly the right thing. There's a famous newsclip of him partying with two rival biker gangs, everyone singing together, former enemies with their arms around each other's shoulders, slugging back Molson beers instead of slugging each other.

"I get it, Dad," I said. "But it's really cool that they asked."

"That's right." He took a sip of beer and laughed.

Then Bernard said, "Remember when you first told us about how you got your powers?" He looked so serious, so grim. He didn't look like someone who just found out they have superpowers. At least, that's not how I would have looked if I'd just found out I'd inherited Dad's abilities.

"You and Mom laughed, said it was an old joke between

the two of you. I want to know what that joke is." I'd forgotten that, but it came back to me now that Bernard mentioned it.

Dad put down his beer. "Sure. It's no big thing—not really a joke; more like a deeply satisfying irony. My powers were created by the Nazis, the most evil villains you could ever think of, and I'm sure they only intended to use me as a disposable guinea pig until they could safely create supersoldiers out of their own men. They meant this power to be used for evil. For hatred. To hurt people. To kill people. But fate played a joke on them. Because I've got that power, and I use it for the opposite of everything those monsters stood for. I use the power to make the world a better place for everyone. The irony of it makes me laugh. I love it."

"You think that's funny. I thought it was something like that." He spoke with more than a touch of venom, and he walked out of the room without another word. I made to follow him, but Mom grabbed my arm and said, "This has been a weird day for him. Let him work things out. He'll come to you when he needs to talk."

But he never did.

Later, we all went out to an Indian buffet for our birthday dinner, and by then Bernard had grown even more sullen. He only picked at his food, even though it was our favourite. He hadn't done more than grunt all evening, and when we were almost done eating, with no preamble, he said, "I want my own room. I don't want to share anymore." He didn't even look at me when he said that.

That night he slept in what used to be the guest room,

and for the first time that I could remember I spent the night alone. It took me almost a month before I was able to sleep normally. Every other night or so, I'd just toss and turn until morning.

Soon after, Bernard stopped sharing meals with the family. He'd take his plate and sequester himself in his room. That year, we didn't even have a single class together in school, so I barely ever spent any time with him.

Starting a month after Bernard had manifested the power, Mom and Dad, always singly so as not to crowd him, tried to get Bernard to talk to them, to return to family life, but those conversations always ended badly and only succeeded in exacerbating the situation. All of a sudden, Bernard hated them both, especially Dad, and he wasn't shy about saying it. Gradually, they stopped trying. Dad, especially, was crushed by Bernard's rejection. The one good thing that came out of all that was that he started spending more time than ever with me, and, while I'd always loved him and admired him, it was during those years, my early to mid teens, that we grew to become more than just family but also friends.

I never saw Bernard use his powers again; Mom and Dad were relieved by his reticence. One especially warm and sunny weekend in early autumn, Dad and I went camping in the Laurentians. Our first night out he told me he hoped that, when Bernard was ready, my brother would ask him about the power, so Dad could share his experience with him. In the meantime, it was just as well that he didn't get into trouble or bring undue attention to himself.

"How long can this grim phase of his last?" Dad had said then. "The four of us have always been such a good team. Haven't we always had fun together?"

At the end of the school year, Bernard said he wanted to go away to a place called Camp Emet. It was a Jewish summer camp, with religious instruction and everything. "Why do you want to go there?" I asked, but he just ignored me.

So off he went, and when he returned three weeks later he had a yarmulke on his head and asked Mom and Dad to sign papers for his enrollment at the Solomon Shainblum Yeshiva. Mom and Dad didn't question him. They were determined to let him take his own path, find whatever answers he was looking for in his own way. Opposing him would only push him farther away. But he was my brother. My twin. I couldn't let go that easily. Every day, even while he'd been away at camp, I felt stabbed by his distant attitude, by his rejection—my isolation intensified by my jealousy and frustration that he had the power and that it was wasted on him. I would have been out there helping Dad. I would have been proud to be his sidekick, to learn from him about being a hero.

"But what about your powers? Why are you doing all this?"

That time he didn't ignore me. "The powers are *treyf*, unclean."

Every radio station, every television station, every web newsfeed reported it. "Montreal hero Hochelaga is believed to have died at the hands of a new superterrorist calling himself the Herald of Hate. This attack is suspected to be connected with the Hegemony of Hate's concerted forays into Europe and the Middle East, an escalating terror campaign that The Mighty are currently struggling to contain and stop."

There was no body, but hundreds of eyewitnesses had seen their hero explode as the Herald of Hate's fist punched through Hochelaga's chest. "Hochelaga had been pursuing the Herald of Hate after the terrorist's as yet unexplained public execution of an unidentified middle-aged woman," the broadcaster said.

They'd caught the execution on camera. I watched it on four different channels, hoping I was mistaken. Every time, I saw the same thing: the woman set on fire by a glowing red skeleton wearing a black vest emblazoned with a white swastika. That neo-Nazi monster laughed as my mother burned.

I tried calling Bernard. We hadn't spoken in years—he'd made a life for himself in Montreal's Orthodox community and had long ago made it abundantly clear that he didn't want to hear from any of us again. Mom dutifully mailed him invitations to every family milestone—birthdays, wedding anniversaries—but he never responded. Nevertheless, I knew his address and phone number by heart. I didn't spy on him, or intrude on him, or anything, but I kept track of him. I had never accepted that he could shut me out so completely. As his voicemail message kicked in, I remembered that it was Saturday morning. The Sabbath.

Bernard was devout. He wouldn't answer the phone—would certainly not be watching television. He probably didn't even know that Mom and Dad had been killed. Well, as unlikely as it seemed, Dad could have survived. Maybe he teleported at the last minute. Maybe he was planning a new, surprise attack on the Herald of Hate at that very moment.

Last week, the Hegemony of Hate, after nearly a decade of silence, had declared all-out war on the rest of the world. Their first act was the nuclear annihilation of both Israel and Palestine; ever since, their forces had been sweeping through Europe and the Middle East. The Mighty appeared to be losing the fight; there were rumours of numerous casualties: Metal Man, Webmistress, Thunderer, Doc Colossus. The Hegemony had unleashed a new wave of apparently indestructible supersoldiers, like the Herald, who was now singlehandedly destroying Montreal, with Dad apparently dead. Murdered. Already several city blocks in the downtown area had been reduced to rubble.

Hailing a cab was out of the question; traffic was chaotic, as thousands—maybe hundreds of thousands—of people evacuated in a panic. But the bridges couldn't handle all the traffic; the city streets were jammed in every direction, and the sidewalks overflowed with people. Bernard's house in Outremont was about an hour's walk from my downtown apartment. I ran—uphill all the way—and I made it in under a half-hour.

There was no answer when I rang the doorbell. For all I knew he was inside but too pious to open the door. I broke a window and let myself in.

Nobody was home. Bernard was probably at his synagogue, praying or something. No—he must at least have heard about the Herald. There were so many Jews in this neighbourhood. More than anyone, they knew to fear the swastika on the Herald's chest.

Still, I might be able to find him through his synagogue. It wasn't much, but it was all I could think of. I had no idea where he went for that, but maybe if I looked around I'd find an address. I started in the room that looked like his office. I'd barely begun my search when I was surprised by my brother's voice.

"I know," he said. "I know every detail of it. Mom's dead. Dad's dead."

I turned around. He was standing in the doorway of the office, with his coat still on. I hadn't seen him since he'd moved out at the age of sixteen. In my mind's eye, Bernard still looked like a teenager, not like the adult I was now seeing. Behind the beard, I saw Dad's face, my face.

"We don't know that Dad's dead for sure. His powers . . ."

"He's dead. Trust me, I know."

We glared at each other for a few seconds. But I thought about Mom and Dad, and I softened. "C'mon, Bern. We don't have to be like this. It's time for us to be brothers again."

My brother gazed at the floor for a second, and then he grabbed my shoulders and hugged me. I hadn't expected that; I almost cried. I was tempted to just abandon myself to the grief, to the comfort of this unlikely reconciliation with my twin, but the urgency that had driven me to seek him out reasserted itself.

Wiping my moist eyes, I untangled myself from him and said, "You have to stop that monster, before he kills anyone else, before he kills us. He killed Mom. He knows. He's bound to come after us soon. He's out there right now, tearing the city apart."

"I won't. I won't use that treyf power. The Nazis created it. It's an abomination in the eyes of God."

"What about letting that monster kill more people? Isn't that a sin in the eyes of your god? I read about Judaism after you left us. I wanted to understand you. It was the only way I could still feel like you were in my life at all. I know about Tikkun Olam: that it's everyone's responsibility to repair and mend the world. Dad's powers would allow you to do that."

Bernard stayed silent.

"And more to the point, I know about Pikuach Nefesh. A duty that overrides everything else. The duty to save lives. According to your own religion, you're committing a sin by refusing to use your powers to stop this monster!"

We were glaring at each other again.

"The Herald of Hate killed Mom. What did she ever do to deserve that?"

Bernard looked away, but I wasn't done with him. Something he'd said was nagging at me. "And why are you so sure that Dad's dead? There are several ways he could have used the power to make it look like he died while he regrouped. I know it looks bad, but we have no real evidence yet."

"I said, Dad's dead. He's dead. The exact moment he died, the energy that gave him Hochelaga's powers, drawn to my own energy, shifted into my body. I felt him die. His energy is with me still. In that moment, I remembered—felt—everything he ever experienced since he gained that power at the end of the war. Already the details are fading, but the sensation of his death will stay with me forever. One more reason to hate this power."

His words hit me like a punch in the gut. And then I thought about what he'd told me.

"You've got Dad's energy on top of your own . . . ?"

"Yes. I'm more powerful than Dad ever was. The increase in my power level is exponential. Unlike Dad, I could—if I exerted the energy—manifest several powers at once. Now, not using the powers is an effort of will, requiring constant concentration. I can feel that filth course through me, taking me over. The temptation is so great. This obscenity is polluting me, and I loathe it."

"You selfish, irresponsible idiot. You could stop that murderer just by blinking. You could probably take out the entire Hegemony of Hate if you wanted to. And you choose not to? Even though your own beliefs dictate that you have to act?"

I wanted to hit him. In that moment I think I hated my brother even more than I did the monster who killed our parents. Because he was more real to me. Because it was so easy to hate him.

People part before me like the Red Sea. They cheer me

on. Some of them cry from relief because they think their beloved Hochelaga is still alive.

The Herald of Hate is easy to find. Downtown is cordoned off by the police and the military. The Herald is destroying McGill University—hurling cars into buildings, ripping the grounds apart, setting everything on fire—while laughing off the hail of bullets and artillery.

What do I think I can accomplish here? Besides adding another corpse to the Herald of Hate's tally?

The police wave me through without question. When they see me, hope springs up in their faces.

Someone calls off the shooting, and I walk toward my parents' executioner.

The Herald of Hate casually throws another car into the air and sneers at me. "Didn't I kill you?" He stares at me with his empty skull eye sockets, and I feel his gaze pass through me. "You're not Kurtz. You're one of his whelps. Good. It'll save me the trouble of hunting you down."

I lunge at the monster, hoping to snap his neck. Dismissively, he slaps me with the back of his hand, and I crumple to the ground. He keeps me pinned down under his foot. My rib cage is slowly shattering.

"You don't even have the power—the power your father stole from us. You're just another subhuman Jew. Not worth my time."

He lifts me up with one hand, his bony fingers ripping through the fabric of the jumpsuit, scratching the flesh near my heart. Without another word, he tosses me away. I soar through the air over several city blocks and crash through the glass window of a skyscraper. Only the pain is keeping me conscious. That and the fact that the helmet protected my head from the worst of the impact. But I'm dying anyway. Blood is filling up my lungs, and more blood is staining Dad's uniform from several open wounds. My ribs are broken, the bones of my hands splintered, my legs—which I can't even feel anymore—twisted at impossible angles. I'm slipping away.

"You always were such a romantic fool, Gordon."

Bernard?

My brother lays his hands on me, and I feel my body repair itself.

In no time, I'm fully mended.

"Bernard . . . What . . . ?" I close my eyes. A momentary feeling of gratitude at being whole and alive is quickly crushed by my still-fresh grief. Yet, my brother is here, and that, too, provokes a rush of strong, conflicting emotions. I open my eyes and look at him. "Thank you. Thank you. I know this is a big sacrifice for you."

Bernard is crying. "Thanks for saying that. For recognizing that. Now you must stop the Herald of Hate. He's a rodef. A stalker. A killer."

"I can't. I tried. He killed Dad. And there are others like him picking off The Mighty overseas. I don't know if anyone can stop him. Or the rest of the Hegemony. He's going to destroy the entire city. It took him less than two seconds to massacre me. He called me subhuman. Flung me away like a piece of trash."

"He won't this time."

Bernard enfolds me in his arms. And . . .

"I never wanted this power. This filthy, filthy power. But you, you don't see it like that at all. You see it the same way Dad did. As a way to mend the world."

"You . . ."

"It never occurred to me before that I could do this . . . but after you stormed out of my house I thought about how Dad's energy slipped into my body. And I knew that this was possible. I knew how to do it, and it would solve everything. I could give you the energy. All of it. You're now more powerful than Dad ever was, Gordon. You have his power and mine, combined, amplified exponentially. Go. Kick that monster's ass. Make the world a better place. For Dad. For Mom. For me."

Clinging to the memories and experiences of my father and my brother—which cascade through me, changing me—I hold my twin tight. "I missed you."

"Go," Bernard repeats.

I fly away.

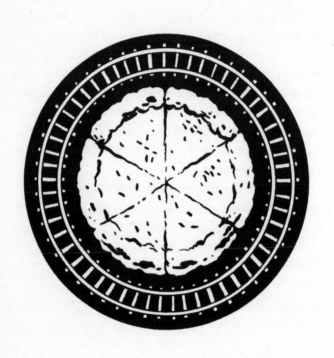

THE SEA, AT BARI

In Bari, the pizza marinara was more delicious than in Rome. Not only did some Roman pizzerias add melted cheese to this classic cheeseless pizza (probably to satisfy the expectations of tourists), not only did most of them skimp on the garlic (again, no doubt to avoid offending tourists' underdeveloped tastebuds), but the oregano was not allowed the time necessary to flavour the tomato sauce; it was simply thrown on top of the pizza.

But in Bari . . . the pizza marinara surpassed Mario's expectations: heavily laden with garlic and covered in tomato sauce from which wafted a strong yet delicate aroma of oregano.

Whenever Mario remembered Bari, a complex emotion—part nostalgia, part loss, part happiness, part dread—nipped at his heart. Perhaps, Mario thought, some emotions did not have names—at least, not in English or Italian. Perhaps it was better to let emotions permeate us without needing to name or fix them. It let them live. Mario felt in short supply of living, lasting emotions. He was hoping this trip would change that.

The only other time he'd visited Bari was twenty-five years ago—the summer he turned five. For his birthday, his grandparents had thrown a party, inviting a bunch of Italian children who could not speak English. Mario's Italian was limited, but he had fun with the other kids anyway. For dinner they'd all eaten cheeseless pizza—at the time, it had struck him as very odd, this absence of cheese.

Much odder, though, were the events that transpired that night. The dream. The hallucination. Yet, he'd travelled from Toronto to Rome to Bari in search of this phantasm.

His flight had landed in Rome—there were no direct flights to Bari from Canada—and he'd decided to spend a few days in the legendary capital. He soon tired of the ubiquitous tourists and the pandering, crass tackiness. All that history turned into a theme park for bored vacationers desperately searching for something to pass the time. There was beauty in Rome—the cityscape as seen from atop the Castel Sant'Angelo; the lush majesty of the Villa Borghese; the piazzas of the historic centre and their boldly opulent fountains; the cats lounging among the ruins of the Area Sacra di Largo Argentina—and, more strikingly, some sort of simmering primal paganism that infected even the Catholic Church, whose Roman expression bespoke a fleshly, breathing, essentially present god rather than the more theoretical deity of Canadian Catholicism. The urgent demeanour and portentous voices of the monks, priests, nuns, and God knows what other orders of robed Catholics wandering through Rome's streets implied an impatient divinity who did not tolerate laxness from his servants.

The first-class, nonsmoking coach from Rome to Bari smelled like the bedroom of a bedridden chain-smoker whose sheets hadn't been changed since she'd died in her sleep, peeing herself as she expired. A permanent stench of stale tobacco permeated everything in Rome and, Mario suspected, throughout Italy. The heavy odour had hit Mario as soon as he entered the airport lounge in Rome following his transcontinental flight.

Despite the malodour, his train seat was comfortable and the service courteous. In front of him sat a strikingly attractive twenty-something Italian, with creamy skin, large expressive brown eyes, and dark wavy hair that stopped at the shoulder. Her beauty was not the bland, sterile look of cover models; her features composed a fascinating landscape of subtle asymmetries. She spent the trip sinuously swinging her head to the music of her iPod. Her face was turned at an angle that let him appreciate her beauty for almost the entire five and a half hours it took to reach the port city from the capital. He suspected that she was conscious of being admired and chose that position to facilitate their unspoken arrangement: letting him get an eyeful while she feigned unawareness and avoided any compromising eye contact. She disembarked at Giovinazzo, one stop before Bari, and let slip a subtle, knowing smile in his direction as she got up from her seat. The headphones never left her ears, though.

As Mario emerged from Bari Centrale station, a pungent yet pleasant fragrance overwhelmed the by now too familiar tobacco stench: the briny smell of the sea, an odour he'd never forgotten. It instantly transported him back to that fateful summer spent with his now-deceased maternal grandparents. Despite what had happened here, Mario's mind often wandered back to that fifth birthday, to that delicious pizza, and to a memory of telling himself, as he lay in bed that night waiting for sleep, that he was having the happiest summer ever with the best grandparents any boy could ever have. He couldn't remember the emotion itself, but he yearned to. He had not known its like since.

There was a hollowness near his heart where his feelings for his grandparents had once existed. His fingers found that hollowness and pressed against it, as if something could still be found there. There were many such inner cavities in his chest. He felt them like tiny black holes that inexorably sucked the empathy out of him and banished it to some void, barren universe.

Mario left his map in his trouser pocket and let his nose guide him. As he was about to step outside the station parking lot, something soft gave under his shoe. An unwelcome odour reached his nose.

Mario swore. Bad enough that his feet ached from walking for three days on the rough cobblestones of

Rome—and now this! He located a bench, sat down, and examined his sandals: the dog excrement had lodged itself in the grooves on the sole of the left shoe. Both sandals were in generally bad repair, anyway. Rome had inflicted as much damage on them as it had on his now blistery feet. He threw the footwear into a nearby garbage can and, barefoot, continued walking.

The street ahead looked like a commercial strip. He'd have no trouble finding a shoe store. He was, after all, in Italy.

Mario located several shops that, in theory, could have solved his shoe problem. However, in Bari, stores closed for a few hours mid-afternoon. Mario had two choices: continue on barefoot or wait an hour or two sitting on a bench in the town's pedestrian shopping strip, bustling with clerks on their breaks.

The lure of the sea was too powerful. He knew that if he waited any longer he would get fidgety and grumpy. So, onward. In less than five minutes, his destination was in view.

The sight stunned him into motionlessness. He gazed at the Adriatic Sea; it felt as if a part of him were stretching out toward the water, as if his skin no longer defined the limits of his identity.

He crossed the boulevard to reach the sea itself.

He had to jump a low stone fence to get to the beach. He was not the only one who had done so. Along the entire length of the shore, people sat on the massive stone blocks, arranged haphazardly, that created a rough barrier between the sea and the land. Some people had cast fishing lines, a few were picnicking, most were simply sunning themselves.

Mario found a small, shallow pool of seawater lodged among three of the blocks. He stepped into that little portion of the Adriatic Sea. The water provided welcome relief from the stinging pain of his blisters.

He closed his eyes and let himself be engulfed by the odour of the sea. It brought back a shadow of some lost emotion. A sense of comfort he could barely remember, hadn't experienced since early childhood.

But just as the emotion was almost beginning to be vivid enough to be savoured, that dreadful memory of being swallowed up by the water gripped him so solidly that, even though he knew he was hallucinating, he couldn't snap back to reality. Instantly, he saw it, just as he'd seen it then: the monster.

He felt again its cold, clammy fingers clutching his five-year-old body, that prickling sensation of the monster's fingertips hooking into his flesh.

With a start he opened his eyes and found himself back in the present, fresh tears on his cheeks—the first tears he'd shed in twenty-five years.

After the pizza, there was ice cream. Lots and lots of ice cream. Chocolate. Vanilla. Neapolitan. Butterscotch. More containers than he could count. As it was his birthday, Mario was allowed to eat as much as he wanted. Excited by the rare permission to indulge, the boy didn't know when to stop.

He'd had difficulty falling asleep when, at midnight, his grandparents insisted on putting him to bed. All that excitement. All that food. All that sugar.

He did sleep eventually, but woke up less than an hour later. Through his window, in the darkness, the boy smelled the sea—so different from anything in Toronto. Not even Lake Ontario smelled anything like this. The new odour captivated him; every day he wanted to go play in the water, but his grandparents wouldn't allow it.

In his pyjamas, Mario jumped down onto the street from his bedroom window. He followed the smell to the seashore.

He scraped the skin of his hands and feet climbing over the big stone blocks that bordered the sea.

He stood on one of the big blocks and stared down into the darkness of the water. Without another thought, he stripped off his pyjamas and let himself fall into the sea.

A few hours later, a bit after dawn, an old man who habitually fished on the shore every morning found the unconscious boy floating on his back. Mario was quickly brought to the hospital, where they pumped his lungs, shaved his scalp, and bandaged the big gash on his head (a permanent scar would form on the top left side, a bit to the back).

When he awoke in the afternoon, his grandparents stood over him, worry sculpted onto their wrinkled faces.

Mario screamed.

For the rest of his stay in Italy, another three weeks, the boy screamed himself awake every night, but he could never explain why.

At first, his grandparents thought the boy was having nightmares of drowning, that he was afraid of the sea. But they caught him trying to sneak back to the shore. Mario insisted he had to be let back into the water.

"But why, Mario? What do you want there?" his grandmother asked in her heavy Italian accent.

In an icy and emotionless voice, the boy answered: "I want it back. What it took away from me. I want it back."

No matter how she questioned him, he could not or would not be more specific. They had to lock his bedroom at night and keep a vigil over him in the daytime, lest he risk drowning himself.

His last few weeks in Bari were uneventful. Mario no longer exhibited the unfailing exuberance that had been so characteristic of his personality. Instead, all day long, he sat and stared seaward from the kitchen window, refusing to play or talk, often simply ignoring his grandparents.

When the young Mario had arrived in Italy, he'd been jovial, affectionate, and playful, but when his parents returned from their seminar in India they'd found a morose, taciturn, and withdrawn child. He barely greeted them. He could no longer tolerate their touch. In fact, he could barely stand their presence and did not hesitate to tell them so, in those cold tones his voice had acquired. Even returning home, to reunite with his friends and toys and comics, failed to lift his mood.

His parents, he knew, mourned the boy they had lost that summer, regretted leaving him all season, blamed themselves for the change in him.

Everyone agreed, as he overheard repeatedly: it was as if he were another person entirely.

The young Mario no longer cared for any of his pre-Bari friends and spent the next several years in isolation. His parents attempted to enroll him in various activities— swimming, painting, free-form dance, jazz orchestra— but they were no match for the stubbornness of their son. Only adolescence, and the consequent rage of his hormones, forced him out his shell. At age thirteen, he began to notice girls: the shapes of their bodies, the bounce of their hair, the aroma of their skin. He dreamed about them and woke up with his groin moist and sticky. He had no idea what to say to these girls, or how to approach them. All he knew was that he had to get closer to them, smell them from up close, see more of their bodies, touch them.

To the delight of his parents, he joined the track team. Tall and lithe, Mario was a natural runner. Track was the only coeducational extracurricular sport at his school.

His attention soon focused on one girl in particular: Lindsay Barron, who was almost as tall as Mario himself, whose hair was so long it reached the small of her back, whose elegant face he could not stop daydreaming about. At every practice, he would stare at her, but they had never even exchanged a greeting.

OBJECTS OF WORSHIP

A month after Mario started practicing, the coach recruited him for the regional competition, enrolling him in the 200-metre sprint. Mario won the race, by almost half a second. His was the only gold medal his school garnered that semester.

As a result, Mario got to know Lindsay Barron much better. And other girls, too. Many other girls.

His first night back in Bari, Mario left his hotel room at 1:30 A.M. without having slept. He dressed lightly—a bit too lightly for the temperature, but he did not want to be encumbered by too many clothes.

Quickly, he made his way to the shoreline. He climbed on the blocks and looked around. Bari was deserted at this hour. Good.

He stripped.

Below him, the sea beckoned.

He hesitated for hours, fear holding him back. He had lost part of himself the last time he'd ventured into these waters. What made him believe he could regain whatever he had lost by immersing himself again? What if he lost more of himself?

Or, worse, what if nothing changed?

Before the first hints of dawn brightened the sky, he put his clothes back on. By then, Mario was shivering. Whether from fear or from cold, he could not tell.

Nearly thirty years old, Mario lived alone. He no longer spoke to his family. He hadn't even seen his mother and father since his eighteenth birthday; he methodically ignored their repeated attempts at contact. Call display was such a useful tool.

Once, for three months, he had lived with a girl: Valérie, a French immigrant whose accent he'd found charming. Her long legs, also, had not escaped his notice.

They were both twenty years old at the time. But, like all the high-school and college girls before her, she soon grew irritated with Mario.

He would not hold hands with her when they walked. He insisted on separate bedrooms. He never asked any questions about her life, her dreams, her days. Unless they were having sex, he rarely touched her at all.

Never before had he lived in such close quarters with anyone, and he resented the incessant intrusion on his solitude that resulted from life within a couple.

It wasn't that Mario disliked Valérie, but, save for her physical beauty, which he enjoyed admiring, and for her usefulness in satisfying his sexual needs, there was nothing about her that held his attention. In that, she was not unique. Mario showed no curiosity about anyone at all—ever.

His second night in Bari, Mario spent in bed, but not asleep. He cursed himself for his cowardice. Why had he come all this way, if not to jump in the sea? To return to the spot where everything had changed for the worse?

His exhausted body finally succumbed soon after sunrise. Mario had spent forty-eight hours without sleep.

He woke at midnight, refreshed and reinvigorated, after seventeen hours of slumber.

After the inevitable breakup with Valérie, Mario's success with girls faltered. When he graduated college, he stopped seeing girls altogether. Not because he was no longer interested in having sex with them—he still found them beautiful—but he had never been the one to make the advances. They had come to him: attracted by his fit body, his athletic prowess, his height, his thick dark hair, his full lips. With Mario removed from the bustle of school life, such opportunities disappeared.

Routine settled over his life: he jogged in the morning; went to work as a clerk at City Hall during the day, stopped by the grocery store on the way home, cooked his dinner, read in the evening, and masturbated to internet porn before dropping off to sleep. Weekends and holidays were much the same, with household chores or outings to museums and art galleries to fill the daytime hours.

Occasionally, when Mario heard people converse, he would marvel at how they seemed so involved in what their companions were saying. He wondered what it was that made them so interested in each other, and he felt momentary pangs of jealousy.

He decided to try. Maybe interest in others came with practice.

On his twenty-ninth birthday, he joined cupiddating. web and arranged a few dates. After a handful of disasters, he gave up. It had proved to be a fruitless exercise. His profile had filled up with negative comments from the girls he met through the system.

"He's cute, but WARNING: he's, like, the dullest guy EVER!"

"He NEVER asked a single question. He didn't want to know anything about me. He kept staring at me like I was a painting or a statue or something."

"The only question this dumb loser asked me was: *Can we go have sex now?* Like, get real, you creepy Ken doll!"

"What a shame that such a cute guy is nothing but a BORING WEIRDO!!!"

And so on.

The third night, Mario again visited the seashore. Again, he stripped. This time he did not hesitate: he immediately stepped down into the cold water. He was surprised at how shallow it was. He remembered it being so much deeper. Seaweed laced around his ankles. Had he after all simply hit his head and imagined everything?

A few metres out, the bottom dropped much lower. Mario dunked into the water and swam. He followed the shoreline covering every possible place where the monster could have lurked.

Again and again, he swam the length of the area where the incident occurred.

Even if the monster were real, would it have waited for him here for more than two decades? It could even be dead. If it had ever lived.

What had he expected?

While he shivered under the hard blast of hot water in his hotel-room shower, he concluded that he had, indeed, hit his head, that the monster did not exist—had never existed—and that its cold fingers had been nothing more than strands of seaweed.

This return to Bari was Mario's gift to himself for his thirtieth birthday. The date itself fell on his last full day in the city. He had spent a week there. The next morning, the train would take him back to Rome. That night, his flight would take off for Canada.

For his solitary birthday supper in Bari, Mario ate the final pizza marinara of his Italian trip. He also drank three bottles of red wine.

In the middle of the night, he wandered once again to the seashore and shouted obscenities at it, as if he could injure it.

The anger felt good. He couldn't remember ever feeling angry before. He should get drunk more often. Maybe that was all he needed to loosen up those emotions.

No . . . he'd gotten drunk before, and all it did was make him sleepy. No . . . there was something about the sea here. Something that stirred him.

Cursing and crying, not really knowing why he was doing it, he took off his clothes and once more submerged himself in the sea.

He felt something clammy wrap itself around his wrist. Underwater, he opened his eyes; he immediately recognized that glow.

For twenty-five years, Mario endured this recurring dream:

He is five years old. He falls into the water. Everything is dark. Clammy fingers make contact with his chest. Suddenly, there's a shimmering light. It's a monster, touching him, glowing with a sickly green phosphorescence. The monster is only slightly bigger than he is. It has three eyes, and they protrude from its forehead at the tips of antenna-like appendages. Its mouth wriggles like a handful of worms. It has six short limbs attached to its crooked, lumpy body. From each limb erupts a nest of weedy fingers. Its skin looks like layers of bloody and mouldy rags. Where the monster's fingers make contact with Mario's flesh, prickly, needle-like shoots insert themselves under the boy's skin. He senses something essential drain from him, leaking into the monster. Then there's a sharp pain as he hits his head.

And he wakes up. Screaming.

The adult Mario struggled free. As soon as contact between himself and the monster was severed, the glow faded.

Mario surfaced briefly to fill his lungs, then plunged back and swung his hands in wide circles. He wouldn't—couldn't—let the monster disappear. He had to make contact. Communicate, somehow. He needed to understand.

There was a faint blip of light as the back of his hand brushed against something.

The monster.

Mario's hand closed on a bunch of the monster's fingers, and the creature became visible once more. It was about the size of a medium-large dog.

Mario felt that familiar, horrible pinprick sensation where his skin touched the monster's fingers. That sensation of being drained returned.

No! Not again.

He wasn't a helpless little boy anymore.

Mario punched the monster's face. It had only minimal effect. Then, still holding on to its fingers, he yanked the beast toward him and hit it on both sides of the head at once.

The pinprick sensation retreated.

Mario swam to shore, dragging the monster, and bashed it against one of the big stones.

Goo seeped from its fractured body. But still it wriggled.

Mario grabbed a loose rock and struck the monster with it until his arm ached too much for him to continue, long after the beast stopped betraying any sign of life.

What was this thing, this creature? He'd been hoping for some kind of contact. Maybe a sort of telepathic communion that would reveal all. What a ridiculous notion.

He would never know.

But he wanted back what it had stolen from him.

He could only think of one solution. Communication had failed, but what about communion? Rationally, it seemed unlikely to work. Yet, it felt right.

He tore a strip of meat from the monster's cadaver. It

ripped easily. He was surprised by the tangy sweetness of the monster's flesh.

The innards, though, proved to be quite bitter.

Mario nearly missed his train. He jumped onto the closest car, and immediately the doors closed and the train started moving. He'd barely located his car and settled into his seat when the train made its first stop, at Giovinazzo.

His heart jumped when he saw her board.

She checked her ticket, and, sure enough, she was seated in front of him again.

She sat down, nodded at him with a brief smile, and took out her iPod.

He leaned over and touched her hand to prevent her from putting on the headphones. Catching her eye, he said, "Per favore?" and asked her name. Hungrily, his fingertips prickled where they met her flesh.

THE DARKNESS AT THE
HEART OF THE WORLD

As the boy Coro emerges from the Godpool, he sees the tears on his mother's face. She's staring at his right leg, which, more than ever, resembles a discoloured, misshapen branch. Two young acolytes help him step out of the holy water. This has been the most painful of his many submersions.

There are five acolytes in the cavern, deep inside the flat Earth. Their bodies pulse with Godlight, covered in the holy tattoos of the Green Blue and Brown God: twin green serpents coiling up around their legs, fangs biting into the flesh of their buttocks. From the waist up, their skins are densely decorated with stars, suns, and moons of various shapes, all in the colours of the God.

OBJECTS OF WORSHIP

The pool of holy water lies in the middle of the cavern, radiating the Godcolours. The walls are streaked with pulsing veins of the same three colours. The room smells of sex, the humid air intensifying the heady musk.

The eldest acolyte says, "Even the God cannot help his body heal itself completely."

"Put him in the water again"—his mother's voice, pleading.

Coro yells, "No! Not again! Never again! It's useless. And it hurts. It hurts so much."

The old acolyte runs her hand through Coro's hair, and he flinches at her touch. "Don't worry. We won't submerge you again."

Turning to Coro's mother, she continues, "Your son would only suffer. It's never an easy process, and he is too weak to withstand another healing. He's been immersed in the Godpool too often in too short a period already."

Coro knows the Godwater is essentially dangerous. The prayers of the acolytes help guide it toward the desired results, otherwise both body and mind could be altered or damaged in unpredictable ways. Every village has a handful of now-misshapen fools who had unwisely engaged in unmediated contact with the God. Like old Urst, headless, with mouths on the palms of his hands. Or Caralla, who whispers to plants in a language no-one else understands and is otherwise oblivious to anyone around her.

And even the acolytes can't guarantee the desired results, as the pain in his gnarled leg reminds him.

The Moon rises from the bottomless pit at the centre of the world and blots out the light of the Sun. For a brief moment, from a perch on a mountain ledge, Coro the lame espies stars in the firmament, but quickly, blanketing the night sky, hordes of nightmares spew from that same abyss in which the Moon rests daily: the domain of their master, Yamesh-Lot.

Instantly, the strident battle cry of the Shifpan-Shap thunders from the sky. The warriors of the Green Blue and Brown God have come out of the fabled city of Shifpan-Ur—as they do every night—their luxuriant wings carrying them to battle against Yamesh-Lot's nightmare minions.

Wielding their fireswords and their Godmaces, the Shifpan-Shap hold the nightmares back, keeping the world safe from the would-be invaders, those wraithlike nightmares who would otherwise slip down to Earth and infiltrate the dreams of the people of the Green Blue and Brown God.

Sparks of fire and Godlight flare up in the sky as the Shifpan-Shap strike at the nightmares. Coro cheers at the dark wraiths' anguished shrieks.

Eventually the Moon begins to smoulder, and it retreats back into the pit before the Sun's fire can consume it. The remaining nightmares flee from the newly revealed light and scurry back to the realm of their master.

Coro watches the Shifpan-Shap as they head back to the great city of Shifpan-Ur, admiring their powerful grace, envious of the awesome wings that allow them to fly. Once again the sound of their voices booms from the sky; this time it is their cry of victory. Coro tries to imitate it, but his voice is unequal to the task.

As far back as Coro can remember, all he's ever wanted was to feel his feet leave the ground. He dreams of soaring alongside his heroes, the glorious Shifpan-Shap. He yearns to have wings of his own, to battle at their side against the nightmares who hide the stars and who threaten to invade the dreams of mortals.

In the sky, his gimp leg would not matter.

He is old enough to take care of himself now. He knows he is nothing but a burden to his mother. Without a word to anyone, he decides to set out on his own, to finally fulfill his dreams.

Shielding his eyes from the reborn sunlight, Coro limps down the other side of the mountain, away from his home and toward his ultimate goal: faraway Shifpan-Ur, where he will ask the Shifpan-Shap to give him wings of his own, to teach him the art of flying.

Only a few days out, and Coro's belly grumbles. He's been foraging, picking berries, unearthing grubs. But it's not enough.

Tonight, he approaches a cultivated field. He salivates at the thought of lettuce, cucumbers, carrots, tomatoes.

In the sky above, the nightly struggle rages on.

The field appears unguarded, so he ventures into it. He picks a slightly unripe tomato and bites into it; its juice runs down his neck and chest.

A dog barks.

Coro runs. But his gnarled leg slows him down. He finds an old tree thick with branches and leaves to hide in. Coro climbs it rapidly before the dog's jaws can snap at him.

The dog snarls at him from the base of the tree.

Coro stays in the tree for an entire night and day, before he climbs down and resumes his journey.

From now on, he will stay away from tended fields.

Coro the lame is no longer a young man; he is not old, not yet, but his youth is behind him. It is a long trek to Shifpan-Ur, longer than he had anticipated; but the desire to reach the fabled city of the God's warriors has overwhelmed his life. So on he goes, swimming across rivers, climbing mountains, walking through deserts—heading in the same direction as do the Shifpan-Shap at the conclusion of their nightly battles against Yamesh-Lot's demonic nightmares.

Coro was born with a twisted leg. As a boy, he tried to rise into the sky with every step, paying no heed to the ground underfoot. He jumped from cliffs, flapping his arms. Or he climbed atop whatever he could, trying to levitate into the sky by force of will. But he always failed. Always fell and hurt himself. Many called him a fool because of his frequent injuries, so he kept his dreams of flight to himself, not wanting to add fuel to the taunts.

With every fresh injury, his mother dragged him down through the tunnels, to the acolytes, but the Godpool's waters never fully mended his infirmity.

On his seemingly endless journey—the horizon still betrays no hint of Shifpan-Ur—he avoids all company, detouring around any settlement or village or city, so that his thoughts never stray from his goal.

His leg hurts. But it always does, and always has.

One morning, for the first time, Coro, now a mature man nearing old age, sees the Shifpan-Shap descend at the end their journey back to Shifpan-Ur. He cannot see the city itself—not yet—but he rejoices at the first evidence that his destination is attainable.

He briefly wishes he could share his newfound joy, but he has not spoken to anyone since leaving the village of his birth, and he cannot remember the last time he even saw a settlement of any kind. But it was long, long ago.

He walks on, with renewed vigour.

Coro, now an old man, finally reaches Shifpan-Ur, and he despairs. Coro can barely grasp the glorious city's dimensions. The city lies atop a high mesa with sheer, unscalable sides. Even if he weren't lame, Coro could never hope to reach even the foot of the wall. Right and left, the mesa stretches out nearly into infinity before it subtly curves back on itself. The impregnably tall city walls are decorated with giant, intricately detailed carvings of legendary Shifpan-Sho warriors of past ages. These high reliefs glow with Godlight.

For one hundred days and nights, Coro wails at the foot of the great mesa. When, in the splendour of the reborn sunlight, the Shifpan-Shap return from their nightly war, he yells to them, yearning to be noticed, but even if his meek voice could carry so high as to reach the ears of the God's mighty warriors it would be drowned out by their cries of victory and by the deafening flurry of their wings flapping against the wind.

Coro dries his tears and refuses to give up. He gets ups and resumes walking, following the nearly imperceptible curve of the cliff's base. There must be a door, or stairs, or an opening of some kind, somewhere. The whole city can't be walled off like this. It must not be.

Coro loses track of the number of days and nights. Both the mesa and the great city of Shifpan-Ur atop it remain unbreachable. As Coro keeps limping along in a circle around the city of his dreams, despair steadily gnaws at the remains of his aspirations, until eventually only despair is left. Until he turns away from Shifpan-Ur.

This is not a conscious act. Coro is no longer capable of such. His mind is now blank as he wanders across the endless landscape of the flat Earth, without hope or purpose.

Coro's parched, leathery skin is taut against his aged and brittle bones. The hair has long vanished from his sunburnt scalp. He has not used his voice since that last morning, long ago, when he cried out in vain for the Shifpan-Shap to take heed of him. If he takes nourishment or refreshment, it is only because his body compels him to. Conscious thought is a habit he has discarded, along with the last vestiges of his hopes and dreams, when he wandered away from the foot of the inaccessible city of Shifpan-Ur.

Coro takes a step, and, as it did so often in his youth,

his foot fails to find purchase. He falls—into Godwater. He sinks until he is completely submerged. His mind refuses to acknowledge the pain that comes with the transformations provoked by the Godwater.

Automatically, still mindless, he swims. He reaches the farther shore and emerges onto dry land. He stands up and holds still; his mind stirs as, stunned, he takes notice of his new body. As the Sun dries the Godwater from his skin, he marvels at his youthful, muscular frame. He is now taller by more than a head, his strong limbs easily twice their previous girth, including his crippled leg, fully restored to health. To better than health.

Dry, and imbued with a newfound serenity, Coro looks to the sky as he boldly, buoyantly, takes a step forward. And another. He has taken only a handful of steps when his foot fails to land on anything solid—or anything at all.

Coro falls into darkness. And falls. And falls—until he lands on a soft surface. It yields subtly under his weight, but its touch chills him.

He cannot see anything. Something slithers on his cheek, and thin tendrils penetrate his ears, his mouth, his nose. Godlight explodes around his head, and the tendrils tear themselves away from his orifices. He is dropped—by whatever it was that was holding him—and he thuds onto a dusty surface. He wonders why he is not hurt, and then he recalls his new body.

He is assailed by whispers buzzing in his ears. As the whispers fill up his mind, his own thoughts and memories are gradually crowded out.

Slowly, his eyes adjust—or, rather, learn to see differently. There are dark shapes radiating a black luminosity, an anti-light, darker by far than a mere absence of light. These radiating shapes, such as the whispering, skittish wraiths besetting him, contrast with the inert matter of the pit's walls and various outcroppings, allowing him to distinguish his surroundings.

Coro, confused yet calm, gets up and walks, surprising himself with the purposefulness of his gait. The whispers are guiding him, wordlessly teaching him to understand what he sees.

Gigantic dark tendrils slither menacingly throughout this strange area, all seeming to emanate from the same source, a source that Coro cannot fully fathom or perceive. But the whispers soothe his fears.

Coro moves on.

He reaches an enormous globe, resting on an earthen cupule. The Moon.

He sees human shapes, their eyes glowing darkly, labouring on its surface. Many of them are missing a limb or two. They smell of decay, and bone shows through their rotting flesh. Some of these reanimated corpses dig enormous holes, leading into the bowels of the Moon. Others climb down into those holes, then emerge from them, bringing forth a dark substance.

One of the slithering tendrils surges toward the Moon and gathers dark matter from a number of workers. It also grabs one of the workers. Coro hears bone shatter as the tendril crushes together the dark Moon matter and the remains of the worker.

Coro wobbles as the wraiths leave his side. They circle the tendril that has enwrapped the dark matter of the Moon and the worker. The tendril molds itself in the shape of a funnel, and they are sucked in.

The tendril flattens so tightly that it almost folds upon itself; sparks of dark anti-light explode from the pressure.

Coro reflexively shields his eyes, but he quickly resumes watching.

The tendril approaches, unfolding in front of him, presenting him with a sword, a darkly luminescent weapon nearly as long as he is tall. Coro picks it up. The hilt burns his flesh and fuses with the bones of his hand. The pain makes him want to scream, but the weapon whispers to him and he is comforted by its now familiar voices.

He cannot make out their words, but he grasps what the nightmares embedded in the moonsword are telling him: he must plunge his weapon into the body of a slumbering mortal, so that the nightmares may flow from the sword and into the land of dreams forevermore, to claim it for their master, Yamesh-Lot.

The Moon rises. Coro watches it make its way up through the dark pit until it vanishes from his sight.

For a time, nothing happens. And then there's a flurry of movement, as all the other wraiths whoosh up from the pit, following the Moon.

Yamesh-Lot wraps one of his tendrils around Coro, enfolding his arms and the sword.

Coro is dizzied by the speed with which he is carried upward. In no time they breach the mouth of the pit. Surrounding the dark abyss is a moat of Godwater—the body of water into which he had fallen before entering Yamesh-Lot's domain; its sparkling luminescence forces him to momentarily close his eyes.

The tendril continues its rapid journey. It rises high in the sky and then crosses above the Godmoat. As soon as it does so, a geyser erupts from the Godmoat, soaking the tendril.

Coro is dropped as the tendril jerks violently, but he is prepared and lands on his feet.

Where it crosses above the Godmoat, the gargantuan tendril that sprouts from the dark abyss is severed from Yamesh-Lot himself and drops onto the barren soil just beyond the ring of holy water. A deafening roar escapes from the pit. The limb catches fire, writhes, and burns to cinders.

Coro looks up at the dark, nightmare-covered sky. He is distracted by flashes of fire and Godlight as the Shifpan-Shap engage in their nightly struggle.

The sword whispers, and Coro's attention is taken away from the spectacle, his thoughts reined in to focus on Yamesh-Lot's plan.

Coro has forgotten his former existence. He is thus unsurprised by his newfound strength and stamina. He runs across the surface of the Earth, moonsword in hand. He must execute his mission this night, for the nightmares encased within the sword cannot survive the return of sunlight.

Coro finds a village. But the dogs are woken by his arrival, and soon the whole village is roused.

The whispers bore into Coro's mind. He yells in pain. He lashes out with the moonsword; he slaughters every inhabitant of the village, down to the last animal. Alas for his mission, every one of his victims was awake; the nightmares were unable to slip into the world of dreams.

Coro runs again, driven by the pain in his head, knowing the torment will end only if he succeeds in fulfilling his appointed task.

The sound of singing reaches Coro; it dampens the raucous noise emanating from the moonsword. Coro walks toward the new sound, seduced. The nightmares intensify their cries, but to no avail. The closer Coro gets to the source of the song, the more the voices of the nightmares are shushed.

At the mouth of a cave, a handful of the Green Blue and Brown God's acolytes are gathered; they are singing, in that language only the acolytes know, their tattoos glowing with Godlight.

The song calms Coro and soothes his maddening headache; his arms go limp. The moonsword drags on the ground as he approaches the five acolytes.

Coro almost begins to remember his previous life, but, retaliating against the acolytes' song, the nightmares now shriek at Coro, driving him berserk.

He attacks the acolytes, but, for all his ferocity, strength, and speed, he is also clumsy. The acolytes move with nearly ethereal grace, slipping out of the sword's reach every time it comes close to striking one of them. Throughout Coro's attack, they continue to sing. Their song changes; it becomes higher pitched, piercing. The sacred ballad has segued into an urgent call.

Coro keeps slashing at the acolytes, never connecting, while the nightmares screech in his mind with increasing venom.

The acolytes' song changes again; it slows down, grows deeper, imbued with reverential awe.

The moonsword strikes something hard, and sparkles of Godlight flash in Coro's sight. He recoils and falls on his back.

There stands in front of him a warrior of the Shifpan-Shap: taller by half than the tallest human; her body covered with golden scales; a prominent beak emphasizing her fierce visage; powerful wings feathered green, blue, and brown sprouting from her robust shoulders. She holds a Godmace in one hand, and a firesword in the other.

She raises the firesword, and Coro knows that it will be a killing blow.

The five acolytes, the Shifpan-Sho, and Coro enter the cave. The warrior has put her sword in its scabbard, but keeps her mace at the ready; she disagreed with the acolytes about not killing Coro, but she reluctantly deferred to their judgement. With her free hand, she holds both of Coro's wrists above his head, pushing him along, keeping his sword pointed upward. It sometimes scrapes against the ceiling, making him stumble, but the warrior's grip prevents him from falling. Two of the acolytes hum sweetly into Coro's ears, keeping the nightmares at bay.

With the nightmares silenced, Coro's memories slowly return.

As the group descends, the veins of Godlight illuminating the tunnels remind him of the frequent journeys down a similar path in his youth. He relives the pain of his numerous submersions in the Godpool. But the chant of the acolytes calms him.

The group reaches a doorway; not the one from Coro's childhood, but similar enough that he recognizes it nonetheless. The eldest acolyte, a very old man with broad shoulders and thin white hair, says to the warrior, "Release him."

Without thinking, Coro touches the warrior's shoulders. Looking at the Shifpan-Sho, feeling the scales on her skin, smelling her foreign aroma, he realizes the folly of his lifelong dream. He could never be anything like one of these nearly divine creatures. The knowledge that he wasted his life striving for something so manifestly impossible shatters him.

She brushes his hand away, and they all file into the cavern that holds the local Godpool.

Coro recalls his vigil at the foot of Shifpan-Ur and the despair that led him into the embrace of Yamesh-Lot. At the memory of the villagers he slaughtered, Coro's heart fills with loathing for himself and for the monstrous entity who drove him to perform such a deed.

Turning to Coro, the elder says: "Immerse the length of your sword into the Godwater."

The two young acolytes are still humming gently into Coro's ears, but he is overwhelmed by a desperate onslaught of nightmare shrieks. He lashes out, and his sword cuts into the eldest acolyte.

The Shifpan-Sho warrior strikes Coro with the back of her hand, hitting him on the jaw, knocking him down. She brings up her mace to strike Coro dead, but she hesitates, her eyes reflecting the Godlight that floods the chamber, and she stands down. She steps on Coro's sword wrist, puts her weight into it, stopping short of breaking the bones, and says, "I should have killed you outside."

Coro is crying, hating himself for being nothing more than an instrument of Yamesh-Lot. He wants the warrior to kill him.

The two young acolytes bend down to Coro's ears and resume their song.

Blood flows freely from the elder acolyte's shoulder. Already infection is setting in; the skin around the wound rots darkly, pungently. The warrior says, "Get in the pool, holy one."

"No, not yet. First, let him up."

She reluctantly does so, and Coro, his cheeks hot with tears, hurries to the Godpool. Bracing himself, fearful of what might happen, he submerges the sword. The nightmares' dying screams reverberate through his whole body. The Godpool seethes, and Godwater erupts, soaking everyone.

Coro expects agony, but instead he is flooded with vivid images and sensations that connect him to every one of the Green Blue and Brown God's creatures. He experiences their bodies and sensations as if they were his own. Briefly he glimpses his mother—still alive, but old and bedridden—but then the holy effervescence recedes, leaving Coro dazzled, acutely aware of the miraculous beauty of his own body. The sword is still welded to his hand, but now it sparkles with the God's colours. He feels the Godwater flowing from the sword, mingling with his blood, and he almost orgasms at the sensation.

The eldest acolyte, healed, his body having shed some of the ravages of age, says, "Now, you must return to the pit."

It is daytime; the Shifpan-Shap have once again defeated the nightly invasion. The Moon is at rest in the pit.

Coro is flying. The wind whips through his hair. The light of the Sun dazzles his eyes. The Shifpan-Sho warrior's muscular arms hold his back tightly against her chest.

Coro knows that neither he nor the warrior are likely to survive this expedition, but—after he had given up hope that his life's dream could ever be realized—he is flying with a Shifpan-Sho warrior.

He looks down and sees the gaping pit and the moat of Godwater that surrounds it. They have arrived.

The warrior shifts her weight and moves Coro to her

side, holding him with just one powerful arm. She takes the Godmace from her belt, raises it, and nods silently at Coro. He extends his sword arm, and the Shifpan-Sho turns upside down, toward the pit. She flies downward, carrying them both past the threshold that leads to the darkness at the heart of the world.

SPIDERKID

All the spiders in my apartment are araneomorphs, the most common type of spider. The second most common suborder consists of mygalomorphs—hairy, often large species, such as tarantulas. Mesothelae, the oldest suborder of spiders still extant, are quite rare; of the estimated hundred thousand or so species of spiders, fewer than one hundred belong to this primitive family, and they're found almost exclusively in Asia. I've only ever seen pictures. The natural history museum has some specimens on display, but I disapprove of taxidermy. I can't stomach the thought of walking through room after room of victims sacrificed in the "holy" name of science.

The body of the female of the common house spider, *Achaearanea tepidariorum*, measures less than a centimetre, and males are even smaller. Female spiders are generally larger than their male counterparts. The common house spider enjoys humid and dark environments, such as my basement apartment.

There are two small windows in the apartment, one in the bedroom and one in the kitchen. The only other room is the tiny, mouldy bathroom with cracked tiles and no ventilation. The two windows are just low enough that I can, if I stand on tiptoe, slide them open and closed. I like to keep them open, except when the landlord's four-year-old twins are outside playing. They like to lie down on the ground and peer at me, giggling. They're not mean, but I intrigue them. So they laugh.

The whole house is surrounded by flowerbeds, bushes, vines, and trees. The landlord and his wife love to garden. The compost and vegetation attract myriad insects, many of whom find their way inside. Their persistent invasions irritate me, but the spiders feed on them. Webs hang from the furniture, from the corners where walls meet ceilings. I do my best to keep these intact, to make my home comfortable for the spiders.

My father held my hand as we walked through the train station. At the age of six, I had never seen such a high ceiling. I couldn't keep my eyes off it and its intricate web of exposed, carved rafters. Gently, Dad kept reminding me to look where I was walking.

He stopped at the newsstand to get a paper. He led me to the comics rack and asked me to choose something to read on the train. It would be hours to the coast, where we were going to join Mom. As I took my eyes off the ceiling, a bright red cover caught my eye. It was a giant comic book, the size of a tabloid newspaper, but with a spine and the cover the kind of thick stock used on paperbacks. There was a yellow band at the top with the words SHRUGGING ATLAS TREASURY SPECIAL in black letters. Below that, a blue logo in stylized, creepy letters announced the title: SPIDERKID ADVENTURES. In the middle of the cover a character who could only have been Spiderkid himself was crouched, ready to leap into action. A dark blue skintight costume covered his whole body. The suit was veined with a yellow web design. He wore big goggles to cover his eyes. A black belt with pouches and an empty holster hung around his waist. A string of webbing shot from the gun he held in his hand.

"I want that one!" I said, and my dad bought it for me.

I take a break from my term paper. My head hurts, my back aches, and my eyes are sore from staring at the screen all day.

Until grade nine, I'd always believed that I'd become a biologist, to eventually specialize in arachnology. Images of spiders chaotically wallpapered my room. Books on spiders filled my bookshelf. *Spiderkid Adventures* dominated my comics collection.

But then one day I was expected to dissect a frog in class, and I couldn't do it. I couldn't even watch my lab partner do it. I ran out of class screaming in terror, and I never lived it down. The incident ensured that high school would be a particularly relentless hell for me—bullies forcing raw meat down my throat during lunch break, that kind of thing. After that, I stopped eating meat, despite the violent protests of my parents.

I learned that the "study of life" involved killing and torturing, and I had no stomach for that. I didn't pursue biology. Now I major in history, a much safer subject.

I check my email before getting up.

It's all spam, except for one message that came through my webofspiderkid.net domain. I run a Spiderkid tribute website. It includes a database indexing the appearances of all the supporting characters, a checklist of writers and illustrators, a comprehensive listing of every Spiderkid guest spot in other comics, cover scans, and other obsessive, geeky stuff. My passion for Spiderkid has always allowed me to tap into a secret well of enthusiasm. Managing the website helps me focus on that energy, helps me find the strength to deal with real life. My own personal religion and virtual temple.

The message is from a lawyer called Laurent Tavernier. It's a legal warning that I must remove my website, cease-and-desist from posting, publishing, and/or distributing any of its contents, and cede ownership of the domain name to Shrugging Atlas Comics, the publishers of *Spiderkid Adventures*.

Shit.

Spiderkid, of course, is Steve Rand's most famous creation. By now there have been animated cartoons, live-action

TV shows, feature films, novels, and more merchandising than any one person could ever amass, so everyone knows the character by sight. Even though he'd been around for twenty years when I came across the Shrugging Atlas Treasury Special, he wasn't quite so ubiquitous back then.

Spiderkid is a daredevil punster who loves being a superhero. His life is a complicated soap opera, but nothing ever triumphs over his relentless good cheer. An instant runaway hit in comic books, it was inevitable that Spiderkid would eventually crawl into other media as well.

Shrugging Atlas Treasury Special: Spiderkid Adventures—the first comic book I ever read—is the most prized item in my collection. I've read it hundreds, maybe thousands, of times. One hundred pages long, it reprints "An Amazing Fantasy"—the first appearance and origin of Spiderkid—and six other stories introducing the most sinister members of his rogues' gallery: "Duel with the Carrion Crow," "The Strange Threat of Professor Squid," "The Face of the Reptile," "And Call Him the Electric Man," "The Mystery of Mister Menace," and "The Coming of the Hellscorpions." Often, if I'm too tired to read when I go to bed, I'll take out the treasury and just browse through it to admire Rand's artwork and to recapture the feeling of excitement and discovery that filled me as I rode on the train, exposed for the first time to Rand's imagination. Exposed for the first time to the mysteries of spiders.

I should be working on my history paper, but I'm too irritated and shaken by the email from the Shrugging Atlas lawyer to write anything. I guess I have no choice but to abandon the website. Damn. I put so much work into it. I can't afford to go up against corporate lawyers; anyway, I don't want to fight. The website was supposed to be for fun, and that one email is the needle that burst the bubble. I take a quick shower to clear my head. I decide to go out.

I blow-dry my shoulder-length black hair, and I smile at the blond streaks—the contrast of yellow against black a reminder of Spiderkid's costume. I brush it back and keep it in place with gel. I carefully apply a thin line of black eyeliner to highlight my dark blue eyes. I learned from my cousin how to make it look natural. She used to tease me about how much she loved the colour of my eyes . . . at least until her parents caught us making out when we were thirteen. Both sets of parents went absolutely crazy. Mine threatened me with boarding school, throwing out all my comics, and getting rid of all my spider stuff if they discovered that Marie and I ever did as much as exchange another email. And Marie's parents were always stricter than mine; I can only imagine how bad it was for her. I haven't even spoken to her since then. I hear she has a boyfriend now.

I dress entirely in black, and I clasp a gold chain around my neck. It's a handmade necklace by an African artist; on it hangs a jewelled effigy of Nyiko, the heroic spider god of Cameroon whose mythic adventures inspired Steve Rand to create Spiderkid. Marie gave it to me for my twelfth birthday.

I weep a little, and the eyeliner runs.

Shit. I have to redo it.

I really need to go out and talk to some new people. I'm stuck in a sad, nostalgic rut tonight, and I hate it.

It's retro trip-hop night at The Fly's Joint. I get a beer and sit at the bar. I recognize a few faces from campus, but nobody I know. That's good and bad. I'm dying to have a conversation, but I don't initiate contact easily. I'm so tired of seeing the same reflection in familiar eyes, though, and I want to meet someone new.

By my second sip of beer, I'm already feeling depressed. The place is full of people, laughing, drinking, dancing, and I feel like a pile of toxic waste polluting everything that comes near me. The space between me and everyone else in the club expands, isolating me; even the music starts to sound muffled and distant . . .

. . . And I see them playing pool; immediately my sour mood evaporates, and I'm focused, interested, fascinated. The man is Asian, probably Chinese: he's tall, with broad shoulders, a squarish face, and black hair tied back in a pony tail. The woman is white, with wavy hair coming down to her shoulder blades, streaked in multiple colours. They're both dressed in black: he's wearing shorts and a loose tank top; she's wearing a short skirt with a bra top. Spiders cover their well-defined bodies: their legs, their backs, their arms, their faces . . .

My throat feels desperately dry, and I quickly down the rest of my beer. Then I walk toward them; I can't take my eyes off their bodies, their tattoos.

When I reach the pool table, they're both facing away

from me, concentrating on the game. Boldly, I say hello—but they take no notice.

They might not have registered that I was speaking to them. It's so noisy they might not have heard me at all. So I just stand there watching them play, nervously fiddling with my necklace, biting my lips, hoping for eye contact.

They're both very good players, pulling off complicated and daring calls. Five shots later, the man notices me and nods his head in greeting, smiling warmly. His eyes widen when he notices the Nyiko pendant around my neck.

He touches the woman's shoulder and whispers to her, pointing at me.

She turns around—I gasp, seeing her face clearly for the first time. "Marie."

And I faint.

I'm lying on my back, and I feel the weight of a hand on my stomach, a warm breath brushing against my ear. I open my eyes, and I don't recognize where I am. I jump out of bed, alarmed.

And then I hear my name. I recognize her voice, even though it's deeper now, more confident. On the bed there's Marie, her makeup smeared by tears. She says, "I visit your Spiderkid website all the time, you know."

I start crying. I don't know how I managed to spend these past six years without her.

I'm back on the bed, and we're kissing, our tongues hungrily probing each other's mouths, our hands impatiently tugging at each other's clothes. Marie touches my neck, and her fingers fall on the pendant. She takes her mouth away from mine, and she looks at Nyiko, tenderly caressing the icon. She lifts it and slides her tongue on my collarbone, on the sensitive skin of my neck.

Soon we're naked. Marie is naked. I stand back and admire her body. I recognize the spiders covering her skin: mesothelae, the most primitive suborder.

Suddenly, I remember the man who was with her. And I'm uncertain, confused. I say, "What about . . ."—I don't know his name.

"Sam's in the living room. Can he . . ."—Marie smiles coyly—". . . can he join us?"

I remember his strong body, also tattooed with spiders. I grin. "Yes. He's beautiful. I like his smile."

Sam and Marie are asleep. I gently disentangle myself, get dressed, and walk through their apartment. I see spider motifs everywhere: statuettes, urns, paintings, photographs, even whimsical stuff like wallpaper and knobs. There are intact spider webs hanging in corners and from furniture. I find the bathroom; I pee, but I don't flush for fear of waking Sam and Marie. The shower curtain has childlike printed drawings of crawling spiders.

I belong here. I need to belong here.

I find a pen and a pad of paper next to the phone on the kitchen counter, and I leave a note on the top sheet, with my phone number. I'm shocked when I realize that I'm about to write "I love you." But I don't. I flee, feeling exposed, vulnerable.

OBJECTS OF WORSHIP

As soon as I close the door to my apartment, exhaustion catches up to me. It's dawn now. I pull out the foldout couch, and I drop on the bed without even taking my clothes off, eager to sleep.

But I'm too restless; I can't get comfortable. Then I'm hit by a headache from being so tired.

I get up again, take my clothes off. I get a face cloth from the bathroom, run cold water on it, and go back to bed, pressing the wet compress over my forehead.

The headache subsides, and I feel my body relaxing, going through the transition from wakefulness to sleep. But then my skin crawls with goosebumps, my nose and ears get maddeningly itchy. I'm about to scratch when I feel something move across the palm of my hand.

I fling the compress from my eyes. There are spiders all over my body. Common house spiders crawl into my nose, my ears, my mouth. And there are more of them on the bed, converging on me. Soon, I'll be entirely covered in spiders.

I've loved spiders my entire life. Nevertheless, I scream. More spiders crawl down my throat. My arms lie still, refusing to obey my frantic commands to swat away the arthropods.

There's a loud banging at the door. My landlord shouts: "What's going on in there? If you don't open up, I'm going to unlock the door and come in."

The spiders scurry away. I stop screaming, and I have just enough time to pull the sheets over me as the landlord bursts into my small apartment, wide-eyed and anxious.

My breath is laboured, my throat parched. I try to talk, but the words won't come out.

The landlord's face flickers between embarrassment and irritation. He looks around, and says, "What's with all the cobwebs? Don't you ever clean this place? Fucking students."

Finally I say, taking deep breaths between each syllable, "Just a nightmare. Sorry. I'm so sorry."

When I start crying, he leaves without another word.

I take down my website and email the lawyer to inform him that I've complied with his request. Then I forage for spiders, and I gather them into a plastic container. I let them loose in the backyard. I fill up a bucket with soapy water, and I scrub the whole apartment carefully, getting rid of all the spider webs.

Marie doesn't call.

She doesn't call the next day, either. Nor the day after that. Nor . . .

I finish my history paper barely in time, although I had to miss a few classes. There are notes online, so I should be okay as long as I keep up with the readings. I immerse myself in schoolwork.

I try not to think of Marie.

It's been almost two weeks since that night.

Someone's knocking at my door, firmly but not too loudly. I glance at my alarm clock. It's 2:00 A.M., but I wasn't asleep.

I barely sleep at all anymore.

I pull on some shorts and a T-shirt. I open the door. It's Sam.

"Hey," he says.

I don't say anything. I shiver, and then I nod him in. I turn on a lamp, one that's not too bright.

He slowly walks through the apartment, peering at everything, running his fingers on the spines of my spider books, smiling at my Spiderkid merchandise, frowning at the scrubbed walls.

I stand immobile, watching him. He's wearing jeans, a white T-shirt, and a jean jacket. He walks with grace and strength.

Finally he sits down at the kitchen table.

I say, "Want some tea?"

"Sure. That would be good."

We don't speak while I make the tea.

I get a fresh lemon from the fridge and cut it up in wedges. I put the wedges in a small bowl, and I put it down on the table. I take out two mugs, two teaspoons, a jar of honey. Then I bring the steaming teapot over to where he sits, and I sit, too.

While the tea steeps, Sam says, "Marie was moved that you're still wearing the necklace." He reaches out toward my throat, and I make an effort not to flinch. He presses his fingers tenderly on the effigy of Nyiko. I realize now that I've haven't taken it off since the night I met them, since I saw Marie again.

He says, "Nyiko. Spiderkid. Arachne. Anansi. They're all

degraded memories of God. Of the primordial Spider who wove the universe into being."

Suddenly, I'm impatient and irritable. I ask, sharply, "Why are you here? What do you want?"

"Right. It's Marie. She's been a wreck. She can't sleep. All she can think about is you, and you stay away. Don't you love her?"

"But she hasn't called me. I left my number. I wanted—"

"The way you snuck away . . . and that cold, impersonal note. Marie's afraid that you're not sure if you want to be with her anymore. If you're going to toy with her . . . fuck. I don't know whether to drag you back or scare you away." I look down at his hands, and I see his fists tighten in frustration. "She admires you. She's always wanted to be together with you again. But she was afraid that you'd moved on after that mess with your families and wouldn't want her anymore. Her whole life has been upended. She needs you to be clear about what you want."

I meet his eyes, and I see how much he cares for her. Something breaks inside me; I know that I'm beginning to love him.

We've got a bottle of wine going. The three of us are packing up my stuff; the process is neither efficient nor rapid. There's a lot of laughter, kidding around, kissing, and groping.

We began early Saturday morning. We finally get everything into boxes as the Sunday morning sun rises.

We go out for breakfast, and then Sam leaves to get the

rental truck, so we can move me into their apartment. Our apartment, Marie corrects me.

Marie and Sam sit across from me on the floor of the living room. We're all naked. I stare at the spiders tattooed all over their bodies. Between us, there's a sealed clay urn decorated with a painting of a giant mesothele spider.

It's not quite dawn yet, and there are candles burning. Marie's eyes are closed; she is chanting softly, almost humming. Sam stares hard into my eyes while he talks solemnly. I don't want to be nervous, but I can't help it.

"God the Spider devoured the previous, dead universe, and then wove this universe into being. God has no name and no gender. Its memory lives on in degraded form in human folklore. Some peoples have not forgotten that Spider created the universe, and they gave God a name, made up stories based on their primordial memories but filtered through their cultures. Around the world Spider is worshipped as creator, in either male or female aspects: for the Akan of West Africa, Anansi Kokuroko is the spider god of creation; in the Congo, the name is Mebege; the Kiribati in the Pacific refer to the creator as Nareau the spider. In the Americas, the creator is remembered as Spider Woman: Koyangwuti to the Hopi, Sussistanako to the Pueblos, Teotihuacan to the Aztec. For comics fans, God has become a superhero called Spiderkid."

He cracks a smile, and I relax.

I straighten my back, and I nod at Sam. I'm ready.

He nods back.

Marie is still humming.

Sam leans forward and takes the lid off the urn.

Marie's mouth opens wide, and now she's chanting a high note that conveys joy, anticipation, and awe.

Two mesothele spiders crawl out of the urn toward Sam and Marie. They climb onto my lovers' toes and move upward. The spiders reach Sam and Marie's open mouths. Sam and Marie extend their tongues, and the spiders crawl onto them, then disappear down their throats.

Sam is chanting, too, now.

For a while nothing happens. Then Sam and Marie fall silent, their eyes bulge, and their bodies convulse.

Legions of mesothele spiders file out from Sam and Marie's tattoos. The primitive spiders crawl toward me, subsume my body.

I feel their jaws dig into my flesh. The pain is delicious. I welcome the creator.

NJÀBÒ

Njàbò, my only child, my daughter, walks with me. She is as old as the forest, while I was born but three and a half decades ago. Our ears prick up at the sound of drums. We scan the sky and spot a column of smoke to the northwest. We run toward it. The ground trembles under our feet.

The settlement is ringed by rotting carcasses. Their faces are mutilated, but the meat is left uneaten. These are the bodies of our people.

I weep, but Njàbò is past tears. She sheds her calf body. Njàbò the great, the wise, the ancient thunders with anger; her flapping ears rouse the wind.

Njàbò charges the human settlement, trumpeting her fury. Everywhere there is ivory, carved into jewellery and other trinkets, evidence of the mutilation of our people. She squeezes

*the life out of the humans and pounds them on the ground. The
humans and their houses are crushed beneath the powerful feet
of the giant Njàbò. She kicks down the fireplaces and tramples
the ashes. She screams her triumph.*

*Njàbò's shouts go on for hours. Our scattered tribe gathers
from around the world to the site of Njàbò's victory.*

*Throughout all of this I have been weeping, from pride
and awe at Njàbò's beauty, from horror at the deaths of both
elephants and humans, from relief, from grief, from sadness
and loneliness at my child's independence.* And, like too many
nights of the past eight years, I wake, quietly weeping, from
this dream that is always the same.

Waters is sitting on Cleo's chest, nuzzling her nose, purring.
Cleo's cheeks are crusty from dried tears. She guesses that
she's been awake for two hours or so. She's been lying on
her back—motionless, eyes wide open—trying to forget
the dream and the emotions it brings. The skylight above
the bed reveals that dawn is breaking. She should get up,
get started.

She stretches. It sends Waters leaping from her chest
and out through the beaded curtain in the doorway. Cleo
slides out of bed, two king-size futons laid side-by-side
on the floor. She looks at her lovers in the diffused early-
morning light: a domestic ritual that marks the beginning
of her day.

Tall, graceful, long-legged Tamara, with her baby-pink skin,
rosebud breasts, and long hair dyed in strands of different
colours, has kicked off the sheet, lying on her back.

The hard curve of West's shoulder peeks out from under the sheet he holds firmly under his armpit.

Assaad is sleeping on his stomach, his face buried in his pillow, his arm now stretched out over Cleo's pillow, his perfectly manicured feet sticking out from the bed, as always.

And Patrice—gorgeous, broad-shouldered Patrice—isn't back from work yet.

Patrice comes home from the night shift at The Small Easy to find Cleo yawning over the kitchen table, the night's tears not yet washed away. He crouches and hugs her from behind.

"You look so tired, baby." Cleo hears the smile in his quiet voice, the smile she's always found so irresistible.

She turns and rubs her face against his chest. "I didn't sleep well last night."

Patrice kisses her on the forehead. "Then go back to bed. Let me make breakfast." Again, that smile. She feels herself melting, almost going to sleep in his arms.

"But," she says, yawning, "you've been cooking all night at the café. You should rest."

He laughs and pats her butt. "I'll be alright, Cleo. Allow me the pleasure of taking care of you, okay?"

She thinks, *Can you make my dream go away?* But she says nothing. She squeezes his hand, forces a smile, and leaves the kitchen.

For a few seconds, Cleo is confused, does not know where

she is. Has she been sleeping? And then she remembers. This is the girls' bedroom, the girls' bed. The curtains are drawn, the door is ajar. What time is it?

She'd quietly snuck into the girls' room after Patrice had come home, careful not to wake them. She'd crawled in between them and was calmed by their sweet, eight-year-old smells. She had only meant to lie down until Patrice called breakfast. Where were the girls now?

Shouldn't Cleo be smelling tea, pancakes, eggs, toast? Hearing the chaotic banter of the breakfast table?

The kitchen is deserted and wiped clean. Indefatigable Patrice, again. No-one leaves a kitchen as spotless as he does. She looks at the clock: it's nearly half past noon. She can't remember the last time she slept in. Last night, the dream was more vivid than usual; it drained her.

Her mouth feels dry. She gets orange juice from the fridge and gulps it down. She wanders from room to room. She stops in the bathroom to splash her face.

The quiet is strange. She usually spends the morning and early afternoon tutoring the girls. West must be at the university, Assaad at The Smoke Shop. Patrice, she notices, is sleeping. Waters is curled up on the pillow next to his head. Where are the girls? And then she remembers: Tamara is back. She must have taken them out somewhere.

Just two days ago, Tamara returned from a six-month trip to Antarctica. She brought back photographs she'd taken of strange vegetation, species that paleobiologists claim have not grown for millions of years.

Cleo ends her tour of the house with Tamara's office and

is startled to see her sitting at her computer, fiddling with the photos from her trip. "Tam?"

"Clee, love, come." Tamara, naked as she almost always is around the house, waves her over. Cleo is enchanted by her beauty, more so all the time. Cleo missed her while she was away.

Cleo settles in Tamara's lap. Tamara is so tall that Cleo's head only reaches up to her neck. Tamara's poised nudity makes Cleo feel frumpy and unattractive, especially now that she notices the rumpled state of her own clothes, slept-in all morning. The feeling evaporates as Tamara squeezes her, digging her nose into Cleo's neck, breathing her in. "I haven't been back long enough to stop missing you, Clee. There were no other women on the expedition." Tamara pulls off Cleo's T-shirt, cups her sagging breasts. As always, Cleo is fascinated by the chiaroscuro of the soft pink of Tamara's skin against her own dark brown. "They were like little boys, nervous at having their clubhouse invaded by a female, at having their secret handshakes revealed, protective of their toys."

"Tam . . . Where are the girls?" How could Cleo have thought that Tamara had taken the girls out? Of all of them, Tamara was the least interested in the girls. She let them crawl all over her when they felt like it and was unfalteringly affectionate with them, but she never set aside time for them. She was vaguely uneasy with the idea of children.

"West took them to school. At breakfast, he talked about his lecture, to warm up. His class today is about the symbolic use of animals in politics. One of his case studies is about African elephants. You should have seen Njàbò! She got very excited and asked him tons of questions. She wanted to go hear West at school, and he thought it would be a treat for both of them. Especially seeing as how you seemed to need the sleep."

"I can't believe Sonya would be interested in that."

Tamara runs her fingers through Cleo's hair and says, "Doesn't Sonya always do what Njàbò wants? Sometimes I think all of us are always doing what Njàbò wants. She'll grow into a leader, that one. She'll trample anyone in her path."

Cleo is momentarily reminded of her dream, but she makes an effort to push it away. She jokes, "Wanna play hooky and go out for lunch? At The Small Easy?"

Eight years ago, Cleo gave birth to Njàbò. Most people thought that the girl looked like Patrice, especially because of her dark skin—like Patrice's, darker than Cleo's—but she could just as easily have been fathered by West or Assaad. The five of them had agreed not to do any tests to find out.

Assaad was Sonya's biological father and her legal guardian. She'd been the daughter of their friends Karin and Pauline. Both women had died in a car accident the day after Njàbò was born. Sonya was three months older than Njàbò.

A few days later, a grey-brown cat jumped through the kitchen window while Patrice prepared breakfast. The cat drank water from a dirty bowl in the sink, and then refused to leave. The family adopted him and called him Waters.

At The Small Easy, while waiting for their order, Tamara goes to the washroom. A few seconds after she gets up, a man wearing a denim jacket materializes in her seat. One moment the seat is empty; the next, the man is there. Cleo is seized with a paralyzing fear. The man is short, almost like a child, but his face is that of an old man. His wrinkled skin is a washed-out greyish brown. He grabs both her hands in his. She feels his fingers, like vises, almost crushing the bones of her hands. "Do not fear your dreams. Do not fear Njàbò. You, too, are one of us, daughter. Believe in Njàbò. Follow her." He vanishes as inexplicably as he appeared. Still numb with fear, all Cleo can focus on is how the old man hadn't spoken in English, but in what she assumes must have been an African language. How had she understood him?

Tamara returns. Cleo says nothing about the old man.

When Cleo and Tamara come back from lunch, the girls are still out with West. There's a message on the voicemail. He's taking them out downtown; there's a new Brazilian restaurant he's curious about, and then they'll go the Museum of Civilizations. He says he'll pose in front of the paintings and sculptures and have the girls try to figure out his ancestry. His favourite joke.

When asked about his roots, West never gives the same answer. A mix of Cree and Russian? Hawaiian and Korean?

OBJECTS OF WORSHIP

Tibetan and Lebanese? He looks vaguely Asian, but his features don't conform to any specific group. He loves to confuse people, to meddle with their expectations. His odd wit has always charmed Cleo.

Thinking of his easy silliness helps take the edge off her strange encounter at The Small Easy. Cleo takes this opportunity to give herself the day off from mothering and housekeeping.

She goes down to her sanctum. In the basement of their house, she's set up a studio. There's a small window high up on the wall, but she keeps it covered, lets no natural light in. She burns scented candles and incense. She's comfortable painting only in the dim, flickering light, breathing in a rich blend of odours. Full, harsh light makes her feel exposed. The dim candlelight, the smoke, and the smells all contribute to a sense of being enveloped, of being in a cocoon, a womb, in a world where only she and her imagination exist. Sometimes, like today, she smokes a pipeful of hash, not only to relax but also to enrich the room's aroma. Today, she needs to relax.

Had she hallucinated that man in the restaurant? She still remembers the feel of his rough hands against her smooth skin. His smell: like damp soil. How could he know about her secret dream?

She holds the smoke in her lungs as long as she can before blowing it out. She wants the hash to wash out her fears and anxieties. She wants to paint.

The hash is strong. She feels its effects within a few seconds, a soothing combination of numbness, purpose, and timelessness. She loses herself in the canvas.

She emerges from her drugged creative trance. Hours later? Minutes? It is darker: only a handful of candles still burn.

She goes to the sink and splashes her face with water. She forms a cup with her hands and drinks from it.

She lights a few fresh candles and returns to the canvas. She finds that she has painted a scene from her dream, one of the most violent moments. She had never before let herself depict such brutality. The giant elephant, who, in her dreams, is somehow her daughter Njàbò, is trampling humans beneath her enormous feet. She is throwing a mangled man in the air with her trunk. Cleo notices that she has painted words in the background, including "NJÀBÒ"—but also other strange words that she has never heard of before, such as "MÒKÌLÀ" and "MOKIDWA."

"Why are you afraid of the dream?" Cleo is startled by this intrusion.

Njàbò?

Cleo turns, but her daughter doesn't wait to hear the answer. Cleo hears her rush up the stairs and shut the door. Does she know that Cleo has no answer? Cleo isn't surprised that Njàbò knows about her recurring dream. She's scared, and what scares her most, somehow, is that lack of surprise.

It was Patrice who had known what "Njàbò" meant, but Cleo who named the baby. How had it come to her?

After the midwife had left, the whole family had slipped into bed with Cleo and the new baby. Cleo had immediately fallen asleep, exhausted from the long labour. She had slept deeply, had not remembered any dreams, but had woken knowing the baby's name. "I think I want to call her Njàbò"—it was an odd-sounding word that meant nothing to her—"but I don't know why."

Patrice, who had been devastated by the elephant tragedy and had read many books to assuage his grief, recognized it. The last elephant, a female African forest elephant on a reserve in the Congo, had died nearly a year before Njàbò's birth. Poaching, loss of habitat due to increasing human encroachment, spiteful slaughters in backlash against conservationists, and disease had finally taken their toll. All efforts at cloning had failed and were still failing.

"I know!" Patrice had said. "Njàbò . . . Njàbò is a mythical creature from Africa: the mother of all elephants. A giant with enormous tusks who appears whenever the elephants need a strong leader. All elephants gather around her when she calls. It's a beautiful name. A strong name for our strong girl. I like it." Everyone had agreed. Cleo had pushed aside the question of how the name had come to her. It was one of those unsolvable riddles best left alone.

Now, looking at the name on the canvas, she is more convinced than ever that she had never heard or seen the name before it mysteriously came to her eight years ago.

The dream now plagues Cleo nightly. She is always tired, never getting enough sleep, never fully rested.

She avoids Njàbò. She has begged off mothering. Tamara, Patrice, West, and Assaad now share the task.

Cleo, after all, has taken on the bulk of that work for the past eight years, devoted her time and life to raising Njàbò and Sonya, to taking care of the house while the four of them pursued their careers. There had been that book with Tamara, five years ago, when the girls were three years old. The paintings, the shows, the tours. Of course, they say to Cleo, she should explore that aspect of her life again, let someone else take care of the house, the girls.

Tonight, the house is quiet. The whole family has gone for a walk in the park. It rained all day, and finally the cloud cover broke to give way to a warm evening. Cleo had agreed to go, but decided against it at the last minute. Assaad, especially, insisted that she come along, to spend time with the family. But in the end she'd stayed alone in the house. Well, not quite alone.

Waters follows her as she walks into the living room. She takes down a big art book from a shelf built into the wall. Cleo sits on the floor; Waters sits in front of her, purring and rubbing his head on her knee. She opens the book at random and remembers.

The book, *The Absence of Elephants*, was a worldwide success. Trying to exorcize her dream, which she never talked about, Cleo had created a series of elephant paintings. Some were scenes from her dreams, but not all. She had used no photographic references. The results ranged from photorealism to evocative abstractions. She painted in the evenings when the girls were in bed, asleep. The whole family was extremely excited about her paintings. Patrice and Njàbò, especially, spent hours looking at them, but it was Tamara who had been inspired by them.

Tamara had sold her publisher on the idea: an art book combining Cleo's paintings with photos of forests and plains where elephants used to thrive, of human constructions that now stood in areas that were once habitats for elephants. There would be no words: the pictures, especially in the wake of the global desolation over the extinction of the elephants, would speak in all languages, allowing the book to be marketed worldwide without the cost of translation. Tamara would go to Africa, India, and anywhere else where any elephants—even woolly mammoths—had once lived, hunting with her camera the ghosts of the dead creatures.

The Absence of Elephants led to gallery bookings. Cleo's paintings, along with Tamara's photographs, were hung in cities all over the world, from Buenos Aires and Montreal to Glasgow and Sydney . . . but not in India, where the book was too hot politically. The two women had gone on tour with their work—wine, food, and five-star hotels all expensed. It had been a glamorous, exciting experience for Cleo—and it had forged a complicit bond between the two women. Before then, Cleo had often been intimidated by the beautiful Tamara's fashionable elegance.

The book, the sales of paintings and signed, numbered prints of Tamara's photos, the DVD-ROM, the web rights, and the CGI Imax film had made the family not quite wealthy, but certainly at ease.

West took a sabbatical from the university and looked after the house and the children. After nearly a year of book tours, art galleries, and media appearances, Cleo missed Njàbò and Sonya, yearned to return to domestic life. She came back home, to the girls. For the next few years, she rarely painted. But the dream continued to haunt her.

Cleo now spends entire days in her studio, has even taken to locking herself in. Sometimes she stands silently behind the door, listening to the others talk about her. They assume that she has been overtaken by a new creative storm, is painting a new series, and needs time alone to focus her creative energies.

In truth, Cleo's days disappear in a cloud of hash. She hides from her fears: of Njàbò, of what she would paint if she were to take up the brush, of being in public, vulnerable to the appearance of the wrinkled old man.

The first thing Cleo thinks is: *Patrice and Assaad look so uncomfortable sleeping on that small ugly couch.* Patrice is lying on top of Assaad, resting his head on Assaad's shoulder. Assaad's arms are wrapped around Patrice, one hand on the small of his back, the other on his shoulder blade. "Patty? Assaad?" The two men snap awake. And then Cleo peers around the room, touching the mattress beneath her. She thinks: *Is this a hospital bed?*

Cleo notices that Patrice looks worried, but she can't read Assaad, whose face is even more inscrutable than usual. Getting up, the men stand on either side of Cleo, each wrapping one of her hands in their own. Cleo takes her hands back before they can say anything. "Enough.

This is too much. Go sit down. What am I doing here?"

They go back to the couch. Assaad squeezes Patrice's hand, nodding at him to speak. "No, love, you tell her." Patrice says. "You found her."

Assaad looks straight into Cleo's eyes, willing her to keep her eyes locked on his. His voice is dry ice, fuming with wisps of cold mist. "None of us had seen you for more than a day. For weeks, you've been distant, aloof, oblivious to the girls, oblivious to all of us."

Cleo's muscles tighten up, in a reflexive effort to protect herself. She's never heard Assaad speak in such a cold, hard voice before.

"We thought you were working on a new series. You let us believe that."

Assaad pauses, his eyes still locked on Cleo's. Is he waiting for an explanation? Or a reaction? Cleo wants to look away, but can't.

"As I said, we hadn't seen you for more than a day. You hadn't come to bed the night before. You'd locked yourself in your studio. The girls and I were ready to have lunch. I knocked on your door, calling you, inviting you to eat with us. You didn't answer. I knocked harder. Yelled out your name. Still, you didn't answer. I had to take the door out. I found you unconscious. The air was foul. You'd pissed yourself. Vomited."

Again, a pause. Cleo feels the cold mist of Assaad's anger go down her throat, into her stomach. Of all of them, he is the most patient, the most understanding, the one who resolves conflicts, soothes hurts and pains. How could she have let it come to this?

"There was but one new painting. Later, Njàbò told us you'd painted that one weeks ago, the day West brought them to his class. I called the ambulance. I couldn't rouse you."

Another pause. Patrice fills the tense silence. "The doctor told us you were suffering from dehydration and malnutrition. Why haven't you been eating? What have you been doing? Are you angry with us? Speak to us, Clee, we all love you. Maybe we should have been more attentive. You were looking weak, tired. We should have paid attention. We were all too preoccupied, with work and with the girls. Why are you hiding from us? What are you hiding from us?" Patrice's voice gets louder and increasingly reproachful. "Why did you let this happen?"

Assaad looks away from Cleo, puts his hand on Patrice's shoulder, calms him, and, in the process, calms himself. Patrice frowns, "I'm sorry, Clee, I—I'm just worried about you."

"Patty, I . . ." She avoids their faces. She feels ashamed. Why has she kept the dream a secret all these years? The dream is a chasm into which intimacy is falling ever further from her grasp. Can it reemerge from those depths after so many years of secrecy? "How . . . How are the girls?"

"They're fine, Clee. Assaad quit his job at The Smoke Shop. He's a great mother." Patrice's grin fills his whole face. He ruffles Assaad's hair, kissing him on the cheek. Assaad fights a losing battle against the grin spreading on his face. "We didn't really need the money. It's a stimulating change to be at home with the girls. It's a challenge to teach them, and to learn from them."

"Who's taking ca—"

Assaad answers, "They're with West today. He took them to see the new *Katgirl & Canary* movie that they've both been so excited about."

"How long have I been here?"

Patrice glances at Assaad, then gets up and sits next to her on the bed, stroking her face. "You've been out for four days. It's Sunday."

Cleo closes her eyes. She wishes she knew why she's been so apprehensive, why she's been hiding a part of herself from her lovers. She remembers falling in love with Patrice when she was still waiting tables at The Small Easy. She remembers him introducing her to his family—Assaad, Tamara, West; her family, now. She takes a blind leap. "I've been having this dream . . ."

The Baka—the few hundred who remain—live in the forest, in a territory that covers part of Cameroon and the Congo. They believe—or believed, Cleo isn't sure—that the Mòkìlà were a tribe of shapeshifters, both elephant and human. The Mòkìlà would raid Baka villages and initiate the captives into their secret society. Their sorcerers, the mokidwa, would transform their captives into shapeshifters. The captives became Mòkìlà and were never again seen by their families.

The mokidwa could take on the form of any animal. They also knew the secret of invisibility.

Njàbò is the ancestor of all elephants, sometimes male, sometimes female. Stories abound of avatars of Njàbò, giant cows or bulls, leading herds of elephants against Baka warriors or villages. Njàbò's tusks are so enormous, they contain ten other tusks within them. Njàbò is often flanked by a retinue of guards.

Cleo has been trying to demystify her experiences. She searched the web for those strange words on her painting and found them. She asked West to get books from the university library. She's been reading about the Baka and the myth of Njàbò. She's never cared before about her ancestry and now finds herself wondering if perhaps there are Baka or Mòkìlà among her ancestors. The Mòkìlà are a myth, she reminds herself.

She's been painting again. The new canvasses are violent, raw. When she painted her first series years ago, she hadn't felt this uninhibited. Now, every session leaves her exhausted, yet exhilarated. Having shared her dream with her family, she has nothing to hide. She feels free.

She still dreams every night, but the dream is changing. Now the whole family walks with Njàbò. And the dream is getting longer. There is more violence, more bloodshed. Njàbò leads the tribe around the world. They crush all human constructions. They kill all the humans. Theirs is an unstoppable stampede. Cleo has painted much of this. Now, the dream continues beyond the violence. The tribe walks the Earth in peace. The tribe grows and Njàbò reigns. Today, for the first time, Cleo's painting is inspired by that part of the dream.

The others tell her that they, too, have started dreaming of Njàbò, the elephant.

She leaves her door open; sometimes the others come down and watch her work, quietly, discreetly. At first, she knew, they were keeping an eye on her, worried that she would withdraw once again. After a few weeks, that changed. Now they come down because they find it exciting to be in the room while Cleo paints. The candlelight, the thick odours, and her absolute devotion to the canvas all combine to create a mesmerizing ambience. Even Waters has been spending hours curled up under her stool.

Every day, Njàbò comes, silently, to see her paint. Cleo is still nervous around her daughter, still avoids talking with her. Cleo senses that Njàbò is in the room now. The painting is finished. It depicts Njàbò, the elephant, towering over her herd, young elephants running around her, playing, celebrating. Around the elephants, the forest is lush.

Njàbò, the eight-year-old girl, walks up to her mother, in silence. She gazes at the painting. Cleo sees the tears running down her daughter's cheeks. Cleo gathers Njàbò in her lap. The girl buries her head in her mother's breasts. They both cry. Cleo can't remember crying with such abandon, feeling so cleansed by the act. She hugs her daughter, firmly, proudly.

I am awakened by a light kiss on the mouth. Njàbò has crawled into bed, is holding my hand. Sonya is behind her, quiet, submissive. Njàbò whispers, "I am the dream."

Njàbò rouses the entire family, kissing them one by one:

Patrice, West, Assaad, and, finally, Tamara. She whispers lovingly to each of them, her lips brushing their ears.

She leads the family outside. The street is deserted in the middle of the night. Njàbò turns to face us all together. We are all naked.

Looking straight into my eyes, Waters rubs himself against Njàbò's leg. Behind my daughter, a group of old men materializes. The mokidwa have shed their invisibility.

Njàbò smiles. Soon, the ground will tremble.

A PLACE WHERE NOTHING EVER HAPPENS

The first time Kyle received one of those phone calls, he was getting ready for a date.

Kyle had been attracted to Lauren since the first time he'd seen her, when she walked into Pen & Paper and asked to see the manager. She was there for a job interview. He remembered struggling not to let his mouth gape open. He remembered actually being able to direct her to Mr. Howard without sounding like a monosyllabic moron.

And he'd made her giggle. He didn't know how he'd done it. But he could tell by the glint in her eyes that it was a good giggle.

He'd always sneered at people—women, mostly—who

went on and on about eyes and eye colour. Blue-eyed, brown-eyed, fucking fuchsia-eyed. What did he care? He never believed that it made one iota of difference to how attractive someone was. Besides, he could never remember anyone's eye colour. Once, a girl he'd been seeing for almost two years—Jessica—dumped him because he couldn't remember what colour her eyes were. What kind of stupid reason was that for breaking up with someone? He still had no idea what colour her eyes were.

But Lauren's eyes were a bright brown that verged on orange. At work, he was almost afraid of catching a glimpse of them. Often, when he did, he lost track of what he was doing and where he was. Her eyes made him dream of a peaceful nowhere, suffused with a bright warm glow. More than once, he'd had to be shaken out of it by Cass, the assistant manager, who, thankfully, was more amused than annoyed. You should just ask her out, Kyle. Get it over with already!, she'd tell him.

It had taken him a few months to get up the nerve to even contemplate asking her out. First, she was just too gorgeous not to have some type of boyfriend or something in her life. Second, she was a co-worker; if she turned him down, it would make things awkward.

He'd had to take a few days off work to attend his uncle's funeral. His mom's brother Flip—his real name was Philip, but everyone called him Flip—had been the coolest guy in the family, next to Kyle's long-dead dad. Before Kyle's dad died, the three of them—Dad, Kyle, and Flip—hung out together all the time: went to movies together, shot some basketball, walked around the city. After, Flip was always there for Kyle, reminding him that life continued. That you had to keep having fun. So they still did all the stuff they had loved to do with Kyle's dad. But eventually Uncle Flip had to move out of the country because of his work, and it was just Kyle and his mom after that. Kyle hadn't seen Uncle Flip for almost three years when he died.

When Kyle came back to the shop, he learned that he'd pulled inventory duty. Together with Lauren. Alone with Lauren. That Sunday, the shop was closed, and they had the place to themselves. No customers, no bosses, no co-workers. If Kyle were ever going to ask Lauren out, this would be the time. Besides, in the three months Lauren had been working at Pen & Paper, Kyle had never heard her mention the dreaded boyfriend word. There might be some hope after all. And as Uncle Flip would have said: life goes on. You have to keep doing the fun things in life, no matter what.

They were taking a break—they'd just finished doing all the behind-the-counter stock and were next going to attack the showcase islands in the middle of the retail floor—and Kyle decided that he was going to pop the question there and then. Somehow the words just wouldn't come out, though.

They were talking about what they really wanted to do instead of working in a stationery shop. At least, Lauren was. She spent every evening writing, either film criticism or film scripts. She told him about the screenplay she was working on, a period piece set in the States during the

OBJECTS OF WORSHIP

Second World War, a hardboiled crime story starring a female private eye, while so many men were away fighting. She told Kyle how she always emailed everything she wrote to her brother Jordan, who never let her give up on her writing. She made some money placing a few articles in magazines, in journals, and on websites, but it wasn't enough. She still hadn't sold any of her screenplays. She'd taken this job to help pay the rent until her career picked up. Plus, it was too easy to spend her whole life in front of the computer writing. She liked interacting with people every day. Faced with Lauren's determination and ideas, Kyle felt increasingly inadequate.

Eventually Lauren rescued the moment and said, "Hey, they're showing the first cut of *The Big Sleep* at the rep on Wednesday. The one that was never released at the time. Wanna go? I love Bacall so much. And this is one of my favourite movies. I've seen it, like, twenty times or something. But I've never seen this version." She explained that studio executives had been unhappy with the first version of the film. It had sat unreleased for a year, until new footage was shot to emphasize the Bogart/Bacall chemistry, but, according to what she'd read, at the expense of the plot.

"So?" Lauren asked.

Kyle realized that he still hadn't answered. "Yeah," he said. "I'd love to go." Lauren's almost-orange eyes lit up, and Kyle felt his insides melt into hot marshmallow goo.

It was that Wednesday at 6:30 P.M., while Kyle was shaving,

that the phone rang. There was a horrible feeling in the pit of his stomach that it was Lauren calling. Cancelling.

He picked up the phone, half his face covered with shaving cream and, miraculously, not a cut on him yet. Trying not to sound dejected, he said, "Hello?"

"Hi, son," answered the impossible voice. "I know this must come as a shock, but I need to talk to you."

Kyle's mind raced through a whole spectrum of emotions and reactions. There was a long silence. Tentatively, the voice on the phone said, "Kyle?"

And then Kyle simply got furious, mad as all hell. "You sick asshole! I don't who the fuck you are, but if you ever try this stunt again, I'll find you and wring your putrid neck." Kyle slammed the phone down.

Why the hell would someone call him impersonating his dead dad? How twisted was that?

Then his rage turned into tears, and the doorbell rang. He stomped to the door.

He opened the door to his apartment, an angry scowl on his face, tears still wet around his eyes, globs of shaving cream dripping from his cheeks onto his naked chest, onto his black cotton pants, onto the floor. "What do you want!"

And there stood Lauren, holding out a bouquet of flowers for him.

And she was gorgeous. Just gorgeous. She was wearing a blue jean jacket over a one-piece pastel-coloured flowery dress that stopped mid-thigh. A simple black hoop hung on her left ankle, and her toenails—peeking out of her sandals—were painted a dark orange. The dress was low-cut, revealing the curve of her breasts, and Kyle had a vision of his face pressed close to them. He breathed deeply and imagined savouring their aroma. No makeup to mar her delicate lips, bright eyes, and freckled cheeks. Her neck-length strawberry-blond hair tucked behind her right ear with a purple and orange flower, which emphasized her entrancing eyes.

The next thing Kyle knew, he was sitting on the couch. He felt something wet sliming on his chest, and he realized that most of the shaving cream had slid off his face. His deep embarrassment and conviction that he'd forever screwed up his chances to ever, ever hook up with Lauren prevented him from appreciating the touch of Lauren's hands, which were gently cupping his left hand.

Before either of them had time to say anything, the phone rang again. When, after a few rings, Kyle didn't move, Lauren let go of his hand and answered it. "Hold on a minute," she said. "I'll see if he's available." She held her palm tightly over the receiver and pointed the phone toward Kyle. "It's for you. Should I just take a message?"

Automatically, Kyle grabbed the phone and said, "Hello?"

It was that voice again. "Is that your girlfriend? She sounds nice. What's her name?"

Kyle dropped the phone on the floor, let out a long, loud, angry howl, and started crying again. This should have been a perfect evening, and it had turned into hell.

Lauren picked up the phone. Kyle was too wrapped up in his own misery to hear what she said.

Later—a few minutes? an hour? Kyle had lost track of time as well as hope—his face and chest were being softly wiped clean by a warm, moist towel. Kyle refocused, brought his senses to bear on his immediate surroundings.

He was still sitting on the couch. From the light coming through the window, he estimated that it was still early evening. Not much time had elapsed, then. Lauren had taken off her jacket. Her shoulders looked so soft. She was washing him. Could he feel more pathetic?

She looked up at him—she must have sensed a shift in his posture—and it took all of his will power not to segue into the never-never land her eyes usually sent him off to.

"Look, Lauren, I—I, huh, I'm sorry about all this. My Uncle Flip died last week, and then the phone—I mean, this isn't—I'm not—Fuck. I—"

She said, "Shh," tracing his lips with her finger. Facing him, she sat on his thighs. She slipped the straps off her shoulders and pulled down her dress. She put his hand on her breast and kissed him, tentatively.

Feeling stupid as the words left his mouth, Kyle said, "But what about the movie? It's only playing tonight."

She kissed him again, shutting him up.

Kyle didn't believe it. "You're telling me that everyone knows this? How come I don't? It doesn't make any sense."

Kyle and Lauren sat in a booth at The Small Easy, an all-night café that, it turned out, they both knew and really liked. The lighting was intimate, but not too dark. There was a candle burning at their table. A big cactus-like plant further enhanced the feeling of privacy by isolating the booth from the rest of the cramped café. Not that it really mattered then, anyway. At 4 A.M., there were only two other customers, neither of whom paid them any attention: an immobile grey-haired man staring out the window, his phone lying on the table and his hand resting on a full cup of tea that looked like it had been cold for a long time, and a teenage Asian girl, with more rings on her face than Kyle could count, scribbling furiously in a notebook between gulps of steaming coffee from a jumbo mug.

"But it's true. I've been talking to both my grannies almost every day since it started last week." Lauren took a bite out of her tomato sandwich.

"Okay, so how come this stuff isn't on all the talk shows? Why aren't there TV specials about it? If what you're saying is true it would be on the news, in the papers, and all that. There's no way I wouldn't know. People would be talking about it. All the time." Kyle dipped a thick French fry into The Small Easy's extra-spicy mustard-and-mayo sauce and waved it at Lauren to emphasize his point.

They'd had sex for nearly seven hours. At first, slowly, tentatively, shyly. Then faster, almost violently, flipping impatiently between every position and permutation, trying to experience every sensation the union of their bodies could produce. Then almost in slow motion, taking the time to appreciate the lingering sensations of every touch, kiss, bite, friction. All this without a single word spoken, until, reacting to a loud stomach rumbling, Lauren said, "I'm so hungry!" Another stomach rumbled—perhaps the same one? Kyle wasn't sure whose stomach had made the noise either time. "Yeah, me, too," he said. They looked at each other and laughed.

They'd ordered together, sharing a giant bowl of fries, three sandwiches, a salad, and The Small Easy pickle platter—an ever-changing selection of marinated vegetables prepared by the chef.

"It was on Oprah a couple of days ago," Lauren said, crunching on a carrot stick from the salad.

"Holy shit. Am I ever out of it."

"Actually, I just made that up."

"What?"

"I mean, it could've been on Oprah. I wouldn't know. I never watch those shows."

Kyle was getting annoyed. "Don't lie to me! None of this shit is true! You're making all of this up!" In fact, he was getting angry, his voice getting louder.

"No, no. I was making a point. You don't watch those shows either, right? So how would you know? I mean, I think it's one of those things everyone knows, but nobody talks about."

"What do you mean! What things? What do you have to do with this shit? Are you in on it with the guy who called me? Is this a big joke for you? Making fun of me like this?" Kyle was shouting now. The grey-haired man was still looking out the window, ignoring them, but the Asian girl, the waiter, and the cook all stared at them.

Kyle looked at Lauren, looked directly into her eyes. They still had a powerful effect on him, as if his insides were being realigned or something. "Why are you lying to me? I thought—"

"That really was your dad, Kyle. He's dead, and he misses you."

"I have to get out of here." He got up and took some money out of his pocket. "Here, this should cover my half."

As Kyle left the café, all he could think about was that he'd just had the best sex of his life and that Lauren was the most gorgeous girl in the world. And that he was walking out on all that. Walking out on Lauren.

Kyle's mother sounded worried. "Are you sure you're alright? It's not like you to call like this. Not that I mind. You should call more often. I almost forget I have a son."

That again. Every time Kyle called her, his mother reminded him that he should call more often. And she wondered why he didn't.

"Well, I've got a strange question for you. Hum. Huh."

"Well, what is it? I'll be glad to help if I can. What do you need?"

"No, Mom, it's not that. Well. Hum. Have you been getting, like, weird phone calls lately?"

"What do you mean weird phone calls? Perverts? Pranks? No, I haven't."

"No, not really. That's not what I mean."

"Well, I can't guess what you mean, Kyle."

"Like, someone pretending to be someone else?"

"I'm not sure what— Oh! Wait a minute! There was this man the other day . . ."

"Yes?" Damn! Whoever this was had been bothering his mother, too.

"Well, this man, he said he was taking a survey, but, really, he was trying to sell me insurance."

"Oh. Nothing else?"

"Kyle, just what is going on?"

"Nothing, Mom, I'm just tired, okay. I— Huh. Look. This may sound weird, but when's the last time you spoke to Dad?"

"That's okay, I know you miss him. You were always closer to him than you were to me. I know you were. Don't deny it. The last time I spoke with him was at the hospital. He was on so much medication; I don't think he even knew where he was. He was mumbling something about your Uncle Flip. And then he went to sleep. When I got home, the hospital called to say that he'd died."

Kyle had heard all this before. Even after eight years, it still hurt. He didn't want to cry with his mom on the phone.

"Thanks, Mom. Anyway, I should get off the phone. I'll be late for work."

"I love you, Kyle. Don't work too hard. Maybe you should take a vacation. I could give you money for a trip. Are you eating enough? You should go back to school. You could get a better job then, you know. You should get a girlfriend. You—"

"Mom. I gotta go. Love you. Bye."

After he hung up, his phone flashed to indicate there were some messages. He checked: five hang-ups. He was pretty sure what those were. That psycho again.

Kyle wasn't surprised that his mom had desperately squeezed in most of her usual litany at the end of their conversation. Not for nothing had Kyle moved to another city. After his dad died—when Kyle was fifteen—his mom had tried to compensate for their mutual loss by micromanaging Kyle's life. She meant well, but he had ended up not knowing what he wanted, with his life, his education, or anything. Faced with the seemingly limitless options of school, he had chosen to drop out and move out on his own; maybe that way he'd eventually sort out what his own ideas were. It didn't work. He was twenty-three, and he still had no clue.

He sighed, because he was exhausted and because he dreaded going to work. Lauren would be there. He'd feared things would turn out awkward. He should never have asked her out. He should have let her stay a pleasant fantasy. Someone to masturbate to before going to sleep.

But, he corrected himself, she had asked him out, not the other way around. She had brought him flowers. She had sat on his lap, taken her clothes off, kissed him.

As usual, he didn't know what to think, what to feel.

Half an hour after he got to work, the sky suddenly darkened and rain came down like divine wrath. And kept on going all day. Business was dead, and Kyle spent a lot of time dusting shelves, pointedly avoiding Lauren. Despite himself, he couldn't help looking at her whenever he thought she wouldn't notice. He should just confront her and ask her what the hell all that phone business was really about. And then tell her to fuck off, get another job, get out of his life, and just stop being so sexy in front of him all the time.

Or maybe he should just quit. Get away. Travel. Like his mom had said.

Then again, he could just sulk and ignore everything until it went away. Unplug his phone for a while and not pay attention to everything inside himself that was screaming to him to be with Lauren.

There hadn't been anyone in the store for hours. He saw Lauren talking to Cass, in hushed tones so he couldn't hear. Then Lauren came straight at him.

"Let's go," she said.

"Huh? Where? I mean, I don't have anything to say to you."

"Stop being stupid." She grabbed his hand and walked him toward the door.

"What are you doing? My shift doesn't end for another two hours."

"It's okay, I cleared it with Cass. It's so quiet. She can handle the store by herself."

Kyle took his hand back. "We can't go out there. Look at that rain."

"So we'll get wet."

The sex was even better the second time. She teased him and teased him until it felt as though his cock would burst. Then she slid on him at just the right moment, and he had

163

the longest orgasm ever. When she came on top of him, she cooed in the sexiest way, squirming sinuously, her whole body exuding heaven.

Fuck, Kyle thought. *I don't care about that phone shit anymore.*

They'd come in from the rain soaking wet. One look at each other, and they exploded in laughter so hard their stomachs cramped; they could hardly breathe.

Kyle didn't remember who started taking whose clothes off first, but in no time they were naked and fucking their way to Kyle's bedroom.

Afterward, they lay in bed not talking, sometimes grunting, sometimes nibbling, sometimes sniffing each other's skin, sometimes slowly—almost absent-mindedly—rubbing against each other, until Lauren said, "Okay, we have to talk. About your dad. And I don't care how funny you are, or how good the sex is, you better not walk out on me this time. Or we're through."

"But this is my bed. My apartment." And he thought, *I'm funny? Cool. No-one's ever told me that before.*

"Pretty clever of me, eh?"

In the end, she had just given him a number. His dad's phone number, she claimed. He'd given it to her that time she'd answered the phone for Kyle. Call him, she'd said, let him tell you. And then call me. Call me. And he could hear in her voice: I know you're hurting, but don't fuck this up between us.

After she left, he stared at the number. The area code

was 666. What the hell? And what was with the thirteen-digit extension?

Why am I believing any of this?

Because the world's greatest girl thought he was funny and liked to fuck him, fuck him better than anyone else ever had.

He picked up the phone: a dozen more hang-ups in his voicemail. Shit. He put the phone back down again.

And then he thought: *Every time I don't decide something I end up feeling like I made a decision anyway. The wrong one. Always the wrong one. How had I ever had the guts to move out from Mom's? A rare moment, that.*

"Well," Kyle said out loud, "here's another rare moment."

And he punched the weird number on his phone. He got the familiar "If you know the extension number of your party please enter it now." But it continued, in a snarky: "If you don't, hang up now and stop wasting everyone's time."

Kyle punched in the thirteen-digit extension. It was then that he noticed it included both the year his father was born and the year he died.

He got his dad's voicemail.

Kyle's father had been his best friend. When he died the world got darker, almost too dark for Kyle to handle. If it hadn't been for Uncle Flip, Kyle might not have been able to cope.

Kyle and his dad watched the same stupid TV shows together, went out to the movies at least once a week, shopped for CDs, played cards and board games every night (Kyle's mom never understood why they liked that so much), took bike rides, went camping—they did everything together, they were the best of pals. Unlike his friends with their parents, Kyle had never been embarrassed by his dad. Dad was the greatest. Unqualified.

Kyle hadn't left a message, but his dad—or, rather, the voice claiming to be his dad—called back in less than five minutes. "There's all kinds of fancy features on this phone, you know. Call display and all that. Even email and internet. Haven't figured out how to use those yet, though. You know I was never into all that computer stuff. But, hey, I've got lots of time now."

Could Kyle let himself believe that was really his dad on the phone? Why would anyone go to the trouble of playing such a cruel prank on him?

"Listen, Da— I mean, how can it be you? How do I know this is really you?" Kyle was still precariously perched on a seesaw of rage and tears, but managed to keep it internal. He had to see this through, one way or another.

"I know this is hard, son. I hate to hurt you or upset you. But this can be a good thing. We can be pals again, right? Ask me something. Anything. It's me. Really me."

It sounded so much like him. "No. I don't know. You tell me something."

"Well . . . While I think about that, I want to say that's one hell of nice girlfriend you've got there. She told me to wait before calling you again, that she'd ease you into the idea. Meanwhile, she even called me a few times to keep me company until you were ready. A real sweetheart, she is. Hang on to her."

Kyle felt himself blush, remembering the two times he'd had sex with Lauren. "Yeah, she's great."

"Good. She likes you a lot, you know. When you find someone you love you shouldn't let them slip away. You shouldn't . . ." Kyle's dad trailed off. There was a long silence.

"Dad? Are you still there?"

"Yeah. Sorry about that. Anyway, I think I remembered something, something to prove to you who I am. The summer you were fourteen, at least once a week we played Risk in the basement, through the whole night, creeping back to bed just as the sun started to come up. Your mother would always still be asleep when I slipped in next to her. She never found out."

"That was the summer before you died." It was getting harder for Kyle to stifle his tears.

"Oh . . . and remember that week-long bike trip in the country when you were twelve? The first night, when we pitched camp, a fox cub wandered into our tent, and we fed it some cheese."

"It's really you, isn't it?"

They reminisced for hours. And then Kyle started asking questions. Lauren had told him some of it the other night at The Small Easy, but he had assumed it was all lies, and he hadn't really pieced it together then, or even fully paid attention.

Kyle's dad explained what he could. "A few weeks ago, Lucifer cut some kind of deal with a telecommunications company—don't ask me the details, these demons aren't exactly the chatty type—and got enough phones to distribute to all of the dead. Well, the human dead, anyway. The animals didn't get phones."

Kyle still had trouble with some of this. "So . . . You're in Hell. You were a great guy. The best father ever. Why are you in Hell? And what are animals doing in Hell? I don't get it."

"Hum . . . First off, there's only Hell."

"What do you mean, only Hell?"

"No Heaven, no Purgatory, no Nirvana, no Valhalla, nothing else. Just Hell. All the dead come here. It's not so bad, really. A bit boring, maybe—and certainly understaffed and disorganized—but not so bad."

"So you're burning in Hell. No matter what I do, I'll end up burning in Hell."

"Oh, no. There's no burning."

"Torture?"

"Nope. No torture. It's just this endless sea, only without the water. It's where all the animals end up when they die. Bears, owls, insects, crocodiles, sharks, whales, dinosaurs, people. It's all the same. You die. You end up here."

"There's dinosaurs in Hell? Cool."

"I guess so. They're just part of the scenery, you know."

"So what do you do all day?"

"Not much. For one thing, you never sleep. You can't sleep, in fact. So, mostly, you just hang around. Wander.

Talk to people. The dogs are nice. Plus, here they don't shit all over the place. Actually, nobody shits here. Can't say I miss that."

"Well that doesn't sound too bad."

"I guess not. But the demons shit, though. And fart. Stinko, let me tell ya."

"Maybe it's their diet."

"Could be. I've never seen them eat, though."

"But, all in all, are you alright there?"

"Well, you know, there's never any sunlight. No movies, either. No TV. No sports. No food. Lots of noisy bugs. Plus you're kind of insubstantial. You can't really touch anyone. Almost, but not quite. And it's kind of hard to get motivated or excited about anything. Nothing ever happens here."

"But what about God?"

"I dunno. Haven't seen him. The folk around here don't seem to like to talk about that."

After the conversation with his dad, Kyle found seven more hang-ups. Kyle had assumed that all the recent hang-ups in his voicemail had been from his father. He'd meant to ask him, but, in the excitement of actually talking to his dead father, he'd forgotten. Anyway, this established that the hang-ups were someone else's doing. Who was calling him like that? Couldn't be Lauren; his mysterious caller had rung several times while they'd had sex. Wasn't like his mother not to leave long, guilt-inducing messages. And it's not as if he had friends or anything. Probably telemarketers, he concluded.

It was 8:50 A.M. He'd spoken with his dad for more than nine hours. *Wow*, he thought. *Dad. Dad!*

He called Lauren.

"He's driving me crazy." Kyle said, while absent-mindedly stroking the hood of Lauren's clit. She squirmed and moaned.

"I mean, I love him, and all that. And he really likes you. He likes how you talked to him that night when he first called and I freaked out." His other hand cupped her breast, lightly fingered her nipple. She gasped.

"And, like, I know he's my dad and my best friend, but, geez, he won't leave me alone. He calls me all the time, and he wants to talk for hours. And hours."

They were taking a midnight bath. The bubblebath smelled like oranges. A couple of scented candles flickered on the edge of the sink. Lauren lay with her back against Kyle's chest. Only a little bit of water had splashed on the floor so far.

"I've been telling him he should call Mom. But he won't. He won't tell me why, either. She asks about him all the time." The phone calls from the dead had become big news. There'd been lots of TV specials and talk shows. Mediums who used to claim they talked to the dead were all exposed as frauds. The Catholic Church declared that the voices were demons working for the Prince of Lies (as it liked to call Lucifer; Kyle's dad had seen him from afar a couple of times and said he seemed like a nice guy). The Church's position was that the voices were trying to undermine Christ's teachings, by denying Heaven, salvation, and damnation. Religions everywhere were having trouble reconciling their dogma with what the dead were saying. And there were more troubles. There were pressures to retry murder cases in light of details learned from the dead, although not a single case had yet been brought to trial for that reason. Scandals erupted in families, governments, and corporations because of information from the dead. The stock market was taking a beating. The media was having a ball, though.

"I keep telling her that I haven't heard from him, to spare her feelings, but I hate to lie." He slid a couple of fingers inside her while pinching her nipple. Lauren cried out, and her legs shot out of the bath, splashing water and bubbles on the floor.

"What am I gonna do? I feel so guilty about it, but I don't think I wanna talk to him anymore. At least, not so much. I know he's dead and bored and all that. But, fuck, I've got my own life now." Kyle lifted his hands, emphasizing his frustration.

"Hey," Lauren said. "Put your hands back where they were."

A lot more water splashed on the floor after that. When the phone rang, they ignored it.

While they were towelling themselves off, the phone rang again.

"You should get it," Lauren said. "It might be your mystery caller. One less thing on your mind once you clear that up."

"Nah. It's bound to be either my mom or dad. Guilt or boredom. My life's great options." With a deep sigh, Kyle answered the phone.

"Kyle! You're a hard guy to get a hold of."

"So I heard from Uncle Flip. Turns out he was the one leaving all those hang-ups. He said he didn't want our first afterlife contact to be a message." There was silence on the end of the line.

"Dad? Are you still there?" More silence.

"Dad?"

Kyle—barely—heard his dad mutter, "Flip . . ."

"Is everything okay, Dad?"

"Huh . . . sorry, Kyle. Hmm. Listen. There's something I have to tell you."

After Kyle got off the phone, he ran over to Lauren's. He had so much nervous energy to burn. He didn't bother calling. He just ran.

Wait till she hears this, he thought.

Once he reached Lauren's apartment, he used the boyfriend key she'd given him. The thought that he rated a key made him feel really horny. He stepped inside.

There was an empty cardboard box on the coffee table and some packing material on the floor. Lauren was hooking up a new machine to her TV.

"Look at you! Are you okay?" she said as she looked up at him.

"Huh? Yeah. I ran here. I've got such wild news!"

"Me, too. You'll never believe what happened to me today." She finished hooking up the new machine. Kyle noticed what it was. "Hey! You bought a DVD player! Cool!"

Lauren walked up to Kyle, rubbing her face against his chest. "Mmm. You smell real sweaty and sexy, and I want to celebrate." She grabbed his T-shirt and pulled it off. She gave him a mischievous grin and ran her tongue from his navel to his neck.

Kyle grabbed her, pulled her off her feet, and carried her to the couch. "Tell me what happened!" he said, while he removed her panties from under her skirt.

"I got a call from *Flicker,*" she rubbed one hand on his stiff crotch while unfastening his belt with the other. "The editor offered me a monthly column at $2000, plus features and reviews at fifty cents a word." She reached over and slid a finger up his butt. "I can make a living at this!"

"Babe, that's so great!" He groaned. "Oh yeah, keep doing that."

They stopped talking for while.

Kyle drowsily nuzzled Lauren's neck. They lay on the floor, their clothes strewn all over the living room.

She asked him, "So you never told me your news."

"That's right. I guess I'll just come out and say it. My dad is in love with Uncle Flip."

"What! Really?"

"Yeah, he was worried I'd freak out, but I think it's cool, if kinda sad."

"Well, give me more details."

Kyle propped himself up and leaned his back against the couch. "Well, it turns out that Dad has always had the hots for Uncle Flip, but never got the nerve to do anything about it while he was alive. Plus, he didn't want to hurt Mom. And he's pretty sure that Flip felt the same way. Come to think of it, Flip never did marry or have kids or anything, and he hung around with us a whole lot. Plus, he was always real chummy with Dad. Anyway. So I gave him Flip's number, and he's gonna tell him how he feels and try to hook up with him. I'll feel really good if I know I helped them get together after all this time. I mean, it won't be like they were alive"—Kyle ran his fingers through Lauren's hair—"but at least they'll be able to keep each other company."

"Kyle, you're a real sweetheart, you know." She kissed him, slowly and deeply.

When she disengaged herself, she got up and took something out of a plastic bag. "Remember when we missed that rare version of *The Big Sleep* at the rep?"

"Yeah." Kyle grinned, looking at her naked body and remembering the first time they'd had sex.

"Well, we can finally see it." She held up the DVD case of *The Big Sleep*. "It's on here. Let's watch it. I've been thinking so much about buying a player, and this DVD especially. But I couldn't really afford it. Now, well . . . my gifts to myself in honour of my new success!"

She put the disc in the machine, and they cuddled up on the couch. And Kyle—feeling Lauren's naked skin against his, enjoying her toes rubbing against his leg—thought,

Fuck, life is good. I don't care if I don't have a career or big goals or anything. I mean, I kinda don't mind my job; plus, being with Lauren is doing something. It's important.

As unexpectedly as the calls from the dead started, they stopped. When people tried calling the dead, they got "The number you have reached is not in service." The phone calls from Hell had lasted a month. "A lunar month," Lauren told Kyle. "The calls started on a full moon and ended on the next." Kyle didn't know what that was supposed to mean. "I don't know, either," said Lauren, "but it can't be just a coincidence."

Surprisingly quickly, the world recovered. Already the news was filled with stories "proving" that it had been a scam or a practical joke. But Kyle knew better.

He never did find out if his dad and Uncle Flip met up with each other. *But they probably did, or will*, he thought. *Hell's a big place, but they have lots of time.*

Lauren and Kyle moved in together into a bigger apartment, one big enough for her to have an office at home. They were getting dinner ready; Lauren's brother Jordan was in town and coming over. Kyle was a bit nervous about meeting him for the first time. He was a really important part of Lauren's life. What if they didn't get along?

Trying to get over his anxiety, Kyle said, "Hey! Get this. There were these two guys—"

Lauren interrupted him. "You know, when I say you're funny, I don't mean that your jokes are funny, so you should stop trying so hard to make jokes."

"Oh." Kyle was confused. Was this some kind of roundabout way of breaking up with him? And he thought things were going so well. Shit.

"It's how you are, who you are, that's so funny. Just relax and be yourself. You amuse me in so many little ways. The look of panic in your face every time someone addresses you. The way you always spit exactly three times after you brush your teeth. How you constantly rub your nose. How you tend to lose yourself inside your own head. How you overreact to everything."

"So it's who I am that's a joke?" Instead of breaking up with him, she'll laugh at him for the rest of their lives? Kyle tried to balance the damage to his ego with the sex and all the other ways she made him feel good.

"No, silly. You're charming! Everything about you is charming! You're so transparent and honest. Real and direct. I love that."

"Oh. Alright, then." He grinned.

Lauren sat him down, dropped on his lap, squeezed his hand between her thighs, and kissed him.

And Kyle looked into those bright brown, almost orange eyes of hers and lost himself in the love he saw in there.

Lauren jumped off Kyle's lap when the doorbell rang. Kyle savoured the lingering taste of her lips on his own.

Lauren walked back into the kitchen with her brother in tow, and Kyle looked up into his big, light-brown eyes, so bright they were almost orange. And Kyle thought, *Shit, he's really cute.*

A VISIT TO THE
OPTOMETRIST

When a pigeon chewed out Basil Fesper's right eye while he was taking a nap in his lawn chair, he finally admitted that it was time to make an appointment with the optometrist. The previous week, his left eye had rotted so much that it had fallen out of its socket. He'd tried to put it back in, but there was almost nothing left of it except a shapeless splotch, and he really couldn't see anything out of it anymore.

His wife Judith had pestered him to go then, before he lost his second eye, too. But had he listened to her? No. "Stop nagging me," he'd said. "I still have one good eye. That's all I need. Those eye doctors are just a bunch of profiteering opportunists. That's what they are. Shame on them. Taking advantage of people's basic needs."

Judith had hemmed and hawed, knowing that there was no swaying her beloved Basil when he got going on one of his rants. Really, there wasn't a political maggot in his body. He was just cheap and lazy, but he always justified it with some highfalutin reason. But now he was blind, because he hadn't listened to her. Although she loved him dearly, she couldn't resist poking fun at him, letting him bang into walls, moving furniture so he'd stumble into it.

"You think you're so smart! Did you ever stop to think that if I'd gone to the eye doctor last week, that maybe the pigeon would have eaten my new left eye along with my old right eye, and I would've paid for a new eye that lasted only a week? And maybe then we wouldn't have enough money left for that intestine shawl you've been ogling at the mall. Did you think of that?"

Judith had to admit that Basil had a point there. Sure, he was cheap and lazy, but he wasn't stupid. And she did want that shawl. She hadn't bought it for herself yet, because she suspected that it was going to be Basil's gift to her for their wedding anniversary. That was in only three weeks, and she still had so much planning to do for the party.

Judith didn't like to drive, so she asked their neighbour George if he'd take her and Basil to the optometrist. Strictly speaking, Judith didn't really need to go, but she knew that choosing the right eyes required a woman's touch. At least in Basil's case. George and Raymond next door certainly did fine without a woman.

George agreed to take them, and the very next day he drove the four of them to the mall, where the optometrist kept his office. Raymond came along, too. "George and I need to look for some new curtains. We're tired of our Caucasians. It's such a bland colour, don't you think? Besides, it's been ages since we bought new ones. The hides are starting to show some wear. We were thinking some shade of Negro. But not too dark. Some kind of creamy chocolate mix. It's a bit more expensive, but it'll look nice. And it won't stain as easily."

Judith enthusiastically agreed with Raymond, but she was just being neighbourly. She was a traditionalist, always had been. Caucasian curtains were right and proper. Though Asians looked good in a kitchen. She herself had Thai curtains in her kitchen. A hint of daring was still acceptable.

At the mall, the two couples went their separate ways, arranging to meet in one hour at the food court, next to the Deep Fried Brain Nugget Hut. Judith liked their neighbours, but she was glad they weren't tagging along to the optometrist. She didn't want anyone else getting in the way of her choosing exactly the right eyes for George.

Doctor Browning showed them (well, he showed her; Basil still couldn't see anything) dozens of eyes in their clear-liquid preserving jars, but Judith wasn't pleased by any of them. Especially with their anniversary coming, she wanted Basil to look really sharp.

And then she spotted a pair in a locked case behind the counter. She'd never seen eyes like those before. The irises were absolute black—or was that just a trick of the shadows?

"Can I see those?" she asked Doctor Browning.

"Well, hmm, they're very expensive. They're one of a kind, really. They were taken from a particularly wily and ferocious feral fleshie." Browning giggled at his alliteration. "Apparently he evaded capture for years." Then the optometrist quoted the price.

Judith gasped, and Basil finally chimed in. "Are you out of your mind, Judith? See, it's like I told you. Thieves. Shameless profiteers."

"I want to see them," Judith said, shushing Basil.

They were exquisite. Flawlessly black irises. And not the slightest hint of rot. Basil would look so dashing in these. Then she thought about that intestine shawl. Oh well, maybe next year.

"We'll take them," Judith said, covering Basil's mouth with her hand.

The deal had been that Yamesh-Lot would make Giovanni immortal. In return, Giovanni would harvest the essence of those on whom he inflicted the dark lord's nightmares. Thus, his lord Yamesh-Lot fed and Giovanni stayed in the dark god's good graces. Giovanni used his long life to continually increase his knowledge of the mystic arts. For centuries, it had been a perfect arrangement. Sure, occasionally some do-gooders would try to get in Giovanni's way, but, even at their worst, they'd been nothing more than petty annoyances.

His eyes, once an unremarkable brown, now reflected the dark power of the lord of nightmares: they became deep black pools. With those dark eyes, he preyed on humanity for centuries, enjoying every ounce of the terror he sowed.

And then the meteors came.

For one whole week the meteors rained down on the Earth, destroying cities, forests, everything. Normally, Giovanni would have revelled in the ensuing chaos. But there was a distressing feeling of otherness about the meteors. For one thing, from day one of the meteor shower, communication with Yamesh-Lot became increasingly difficult. The meteors were generating some kind of interference or static. By the end of the seventh day, when the last meteors hit the Earth, Giovanni's connection to Yamesh-Lot had been completely severed.

He could still inflict nightmares and other curses on pitiful mortal fools—Giovanni was, after all, a master of black magic—but the dark lord was not there to accept the sorcerer's sacrifices.

And something else happened on the seventh day. The dead rose.

At first Giovanni wondered why only human corpses were zombified. And then he noticed the occasional reanimated dog or cat. In time, he figured out that the meteors must have emitted some kind of radiation that interacted with embalming fluid, as unlikely as that sounded. He knew that there must be more to it, but his spells failed to solve the mystery.

Magic became increasingly taxing for Giovanni; before the time of the zombies he could weave his spells with almost as little effort as it took to breathe. But now . . . He resented how weak he grew when practicing the dark arts.

For weeks the reanimated human corpses ravaged the planet, popping open human skulls and feeding on the brains inside. They never ate the brains of other animals.

After a while, though, the undead lost some of their savage fury, and they began rounding up the surviving humans. Then they farmed them. At first, just for food, but eventually the zombies found other uses for the remains of human bodies.

Giovanni's earthbound magics were useless against the undead. They possessed some kind of immunity that he could not overcome. Besides, the centuries-old sorcerer felt his powers waning. Something about the extraterrestrial nature of the meteors and the zombies they created seemed to disrupt the energy flux from which he drew his powers. The undead were invaders, and they had conquered.

So he hid. His magics were still strong enough for that. He hid for so many centuries—scavenging for food, always careful to steer clear of the invaders' hunting parties—that he lost track of time entirely.

And he grew lonely. For so long he had preyed on humanity in the name of his dark lord. In this new world of zombies, not only was it unwise to bring attention to himself, but it was very rare that he would come across a human in the wild. Almost all humans were farm animals. He had no-one to prey upon. And he yearned for the dark embrace of his god. It was inconceivable to Giovanni that the invaders had fully extinguished the eternal darkness of Yamesh-Lot; but no spell and no ritual was ever successful in re-establishing Giovanni's link to the dark lord of nightmares.

And so Giovanni grew insane, forgetting his name, his identity, forgetting even Yamesh-Lot. The ageless sorcerer was reduced to no more than a scavenger who cared only about survival.

His spells of protection eventually petered out. Inevitably, undead hunters found and captured him.

Giovanni's brain was removed from his skull and mashed into puree along with many other brains. His various body parts were recycled into the zombie economy.

And his eyes, his perfectly black eyes, were harvested and put on sale.

For the next few days, Basil complained about the exorbitant price they'd paid for his new eyes, but Judith could tell he was doing it out of habit. Her husband had always been a complainer. After so many years of marriage, though, she could distinguish between serious grievances and mere blathering. There was also a bit of ego-saving in there; Basil never liked being the one who was wrong. Not that he ever got mad or anything; underneath all that gruff complaining, Basil hid a tender mess of rotting flesh. He was a such a sweetie, really.

She caught him admiring himself in the mirror; he really did like his snazzy new eyes. But she didn't tease him; it would only take longer for him to get over his complaining stage.

And so it took less than a week for him to say, "You know,

these eyes don't look half bad. Plus, they feel robust, like they're gonna last longer." Judith smiled, and Basil kissed her on the cheek. He kept his mouth open just enough so that his maggots tickled her cheek. He knew how she liked that.

Judith loved how those new eyes made him look so suave and sexy. She gasped, "Oh, Basil . . ."

And they fell into each other arms. He carried her into the living room and gently laid her down on the plush tongue rug he'd bought her for their last anniversary.

It had been decades—at least!—since Basil had made love to her.

"Oh, Basil . . . Yes . . . Yes . . ."

Slowly, Giovanni regained consciousness. At first, he numbly watched the parade of images that presented itself before his eyes. A zombie woman wearing garish and filthy rags; the suburban house decorated with human body parts; the refrigerator filled with processed brain products; brains being cooked on the barbecue in the backyard; zombies driving automobiles or walking the streets in the moonlight; and lots and lots of television: strange sports he could not fathom, zombie/human pornography, teleplays that defied comprehension.

But, gradually, his frustration at not being able to act on those images gnawed at him, and Giovanni remembered who he was. What he was.

A scourge upon the vermin of humanity. A fearsome sorcerer. A high priest of Yamesh-Lot.

He prayed to his dark lord, but the god remained silent. And yet . . . for the first time in centuries, Giovanni sensed Yamesh-Lot just beyond his reach. His god was still alive! How could the sorcerer-priest re-establish his connection to the lord of nightmares?

One day, while his host body stood in front of a mirror rubbing a brownish sludge onto the decaying flesh of its face, Giovanni recognized his own black eyes—a legacy of his devotion to his god—staring back at him.

For a second, Giovanni feared he'd become a zombie, but then he realized this zombie's body was entirely the wrong shape—taller and narrower than he had been. This monster was . . . *wearing* Giovanni's eyes. The way the creature admired them in the mirror, Giovanni suspected he'd only recently acquired them.

But just as Giovanni began to curse at the ignominious humiliation of being reduced to the state of eyewear for a rotting monstrosity, the sorcerer felt a twinkle of energy. Somehow, being inside this creature's body enabled him to once again tap into the dark forces that fuelled his sorcery.

Giovanni knew then that he could take control of this ridiculous creature's body. He would then perform the rituals that would return Yamesh-Lot to the mortal world. For his dark lord, he would rid the Earth of this unwanted pestilence. Humanity was Yamesh-Lot's to prey upon. Giovanni had no doubts that the reign of these repulsive usurpers was to finally come to an end and that he would be the agent of their downfall.

OBJECTS OF WORSHIP

Their anniversary party was only a week away, and Judith was getting worried about Basil. Since getting those new eyes, Basil had changed. At first, it was all for the better—he was more cheerful and he paid better attention to her than he had in centuries—but then he started acting strangely.

He spent hours staring at himself in the mirror, gesticulating oddly, ignoring her when she asked him what he was doing. He now rarely spoke to her, and, when he did, he was abrupt with her and sounded confused.

She was pondering all of that while stirring the brain stew. Her own secret recipe: she minced two teaspoons of sun-dried testes and mixed it with half a cup of crumbled skin flakes and half a cup of grated bone, with sprinkles of liver powder and finely chopped earlobes, then gradually stirred the blend into the soup. She topped it all off with a tablespoon of fresh marrow juice. The trick was not to simply dump all the spices in at once. Basil loved this dish so much. Maybe having it for dinner would snap him out of his bizarre mood.

This fool is so easy to control, thought Giovanni. This Basil, as he called himself, had no willpower to speak of. The hardest thing was learning to control the pain. Every part of this creature's body sent continual streams of pain into their shared brain. Moving was even worse agony. It threatened to shatter his concentration, but Giovanni's mystic training helped him overcome this obstacle.

Giovanni was learning, also, to access the monster's memories. This upcoming wedding anniversary celebration that the creature's wife Judith was always going on about would be a perfect occasion to perform the rituals that would—he hoped—reconnect Yamesh-Lot to this world.

He would have to learn to be more patient with the decaying, stupid hag. He could use her help. He would have to fool her into helping him with the necessary preparations.

He was confident that he had achieved complete control of Basil's body; he should concentrate on enlisting Judith's unwitting aid.

He stepped into the kitchen, intending to woo the monstrous female.

She stood at the stove, stirring some putrid, foul-smelling concoction.

Judith heard the door creak open and turned to see Basil walk into the kitchen. He smiled at her.

Holding his arms out toward her, he said, "Judith, darling, I'm sorry I've been so distant these past few days; it's the stress, y—"

And then his body contorted every which way, his face twisting maniacally, maggots flipping out of his mouth, nose, and ears.

Judith just didn't know what to think anymore. What was going on with Basil these days? After centuries of marriage, you'd think she knew all of his moods.

After a few minutes, Basil finally steadied himself on the table. He shook his head as if to collect himself, and then said, with a hint of desperation, "Oh Judith, baby . . .

That smell! I love your brain stew! That's what gave me the strength to come back. That wasn't me—"

And then the contortions began again, more violent than before. Basil looked like he had no control over his movements. She was worried that he might lose an arm or something. The last thing they needed was the expense of reconstructive surgery. What was wrong with that man!

Judith had to duck out the back door to avoid being hit by Basil's flailing body. She peered inside through the window, mesmerized by the strange and disturbing spectacle. Nearly fifteen minutes later, the episode finally subsided, and Basil collapsed on the floor.

Giovanni had underestimated the strength of the monster's willpower. While he and Basil struggled for control, the body lay paralyzed on the kitchen floor.

I am Giovanni, high priest of the redoubtable Yamesh-Lot; you are nothing but a snivelling abomination, the sorcerer mentally spat at Basil.

Oh yeah! Well, you're nothing but a filthy fleshie animal. I eat dumb beasts like you for breakfast, Basil spat right back.

You cannot hope to match the power of my eldritch magics, monster. You will succumb, and I will triumph.

This is my body, and I'm not gonna let some stupid animal control me.

Cringe before my might, vile monster!

And so it went, for interminable hours.

Judith called Doctor Dora. She'd been their family

physician for ages, and she was one of the rare doctors who still made house calls. It was the only way Judith ever got Basil close to having a checkup. He didn't trust doctors, but good old Doctor Dora always took his jibes with a grin. He never let her give him a physical or directly examine him in any way, but she knew how to surreptitiously ask the right questions.

After she left a message with Doctor Dora's secretary, Judith cleaned the mess Basil had made in the kitchen. While he was flailing madly, he'd knocked the pot from the stove, splattering Judith's brain stew all over the kitchen.

It was a shame that so much food had been wasted, but she noted with pleasure how the stew seeped into the fleshly plush of the chairs, how it filtered through cracks where the counter met the wall. At least the kitchen would always keep a fresh aroma of decaying brains. Judith liked to see the positive side of things.

It was hard to clean the floor, though, what with Basil just lying there. So she dragged him into the living room. As she did so, she noticed how the stew that had spilled on him was leaving a trail of brain slime. She plopped him on the couch, and, as she'd hoped, she saw brain stains appear on the upholstery. The living room would smell really brainy now. The positive! Always concentrate on the positive!

As Judith was about to return to the kitchen, the doorbell rang. *That was fast*, thought Judith. *Good old Doctor Dora!*

But it was their neighbour Raymond at the door. "Hello, Judith, dear. I'm so sorry to be barging in like this, but I was wondering if I could borrow a cup of brain butter? I need it for dinner tonight, and I hadn't realized that we were out."

"Huh—"

"Mmm. Is that your brain stew I'm smelling? You know, you've never given me that recipe."

"I—"

"Judith, dear. How rude of me! You must be exhausted. All those preparations for the big party."

"Basil is . . . I mean . . . Yes, I've got some brain butter. Just come in the kitchen." Judith had no time to deal with Raymond. How that man could natter! Couldn't he see she was in the middle of a crisis, here?

On his way to the kitchen, Raymond noticed Basil on the couch. "Still the same old Basil! Napping while you run yourself ragged. You should whip that man into shape sometime, Judith, dear."

Judith's patience had just about run out. She opened her mouth to give her neighbour a piece of her mind, but Raymond was saved by the doorbell.

Judith had hoped to get Raymond out before the doctor arrived. She didn't want him to gossip about Basil's health, especially now, when all she wanted was a nice anniversary party without having to worry what people said about her and Basil behind their backs. Maybe she could shoo him out the back door?

"Raymond, dear, could you maybe get the butter yourself and see yourself out by the back? As you said, I'm so dreadfully busy, and that would help me." The doorbell rang again.

"Of course, Judith. So sorry." Raymond gently patted

Judith's arm; it took all her self-control not to sock him one.

As he headed for the kitchen, Judith opened the door on the third ring. This time it really was Doctor Dora.

The war between Giovanni and Basil raged on, with no victor in sight.

After Doctor Dora left, Judith's anxiety grew. The doctor had recommended hospital care, and Judith knew that Basil would just hate that. She'd told the doctor that she'd have to think about it.

The problem was that Doctor Dora had not been able to diagnose Basil. As far as the doctor could tell, there was nothing wrong with Basil. She couldn't explain why he was unconscious and unresponsive.

Responsive! That word sparked an idea. Basil loved her brain stew so much. There was still some left in the pot. What if she fed him some? Maybe that would bring him out of it. It certainly couldn't hurt.

It seemed like nothing could break the stalemate. Giovanni had sorcerous might on his side, but Basil had the advantage of fighting on his home turf, his own body.

And then Judith poured some brain stew down Basil's throat.

Basil's favourite dish. The taste distracted him for a split second, and that was just enough for Giovanni to gain the advantage and push Basil's conscience down into some dim cellar of the mind the two now shared. Giovanni could have obliterated Basil completely, but he was afraid of the consequences. He might inadvertently kill himself in the process.

Giovanni regained control. He stirred Basil's body awake.

When Basil regained consciousness, Judith started asking him questions, but he shushed her, saying, "I'm just so nervous and excited about our anniversary, baby; it's making me realize how much you mean to me."

And then he kissed her, almost shyly, like he'd never done it before.

Well this was one change she didn't mind. Basil had never been so romantic before. Talking about their anniversary that way, and then that tender kiss, his mouth maggots tickling her lips. Those new eyes of his had really made a difference. She hoped they'd last, or at least have a lasting effect!

Then he picked her up in his arms and led her to the bedroom.

In all his years of service to the dark lord Yamesh-Lot, never had Giovanni been called upon to do something as disgusting as having sex with a zombie in a bed of mud.

He had to admit, though, that the mud felt really good, soothing his decaying flesh. These zombies appeared to be immortal, and somehow they regenerated skin and organs just fast enough to keep most of their skeletal frames covered, but not so fast as to lose that permanent veneer of putrid decay.

When he'd pressed his maggot-filled mouth onto Judith's maggot-filled vulva, it required all his self-discipline to keep up his role as the enthusiastically enamoured Basil.

Afterward, he'd told her how he wanted to decorate the backyard for the party "so it would be just perfect," and what could she do but agree?

Judith couldn't remember Basil ever having been so assertive before. At first she'd enjoyed how he was showing so much interest in their anniversary party. She fell in love with him all over again.

But then, despite herself, she started to resent him. He grew increasingly bossy, insisting that things be exactly the way he wanted them. If she showed any hesitation, he'd start having sex with her with such vigour that she found herself unable to deny him anything.

She couldn't recognize her husband or her marriage, torn between missing the comfort of how things had always been and thrilling at the excitement of Basil's newfound virility and unpredictability.

Of all Giovanni's preparations for summoning Yamesh-Lot back to this plane of existence, the torches laid out in the shape of a star was the one he'd had to work the hardest to convince Judith to accept. She just didn't like fire—was quite afraid of it, in fact. Maybe these creatures were particularly vulnerable to fire? In any case, after a weekend outing at a fleshie slaughterhouse—where, for a fee, you could watch a zombie butcher rip apart live humans and, if you were lucky, maybe even get splattered by a bit of gore—followed by a five-hour sex session next to a lake of raw sewage, she finally relented.

Judith wanted to be loved, and Giovanni was grateful that Basil had done such a poor job of it all these centuries. It made his work easier now.

So the big day was finally here. The guests had started to file into the backyard, the torches had been lit in the proper order, the animal skins had been hung just right, the appropriate mystical sigils had been painted on the available surfaces.

These abominations wanted a party. He'd show them a good time.

George and Raymond were the last of the guests to arrive. "Happy anniversary!" Raymond squealed while George handed Judith their gift.

Judith gracefully accepted the Negro curtains from George and Raymond. "Did you guess that we were sounding you out that day at the mall?" Raymond asked. "We were so thrilled that you liked this shade."

Maybe she could "accidentally" burn these curtains or something? Maybe Basil's torches would be good for something after all? There was no way she was going to put these up in her house.

Biting down her irritation, Judith disentangled herself from her neighbours to see how Basil was dealing with the guests.

Why was Basil embarrassing her so? Yes, Judith liked all the sex and romance in their lives nowadays, but she had to admit that, in the end, she'd made up her mind that she preferred the old Basil. The one she could predict. The one she could control. The one who wasn't so weird.

Basil lined up the confused guests in a spiral around the torches. He asked them to join hands; he was so excited it was as if he were standing in front of an open vat of fresh brains.

Basil waved to Judith, "Come on, darling! The fun's about to start!"

Yes! Giovanni sensed Yamesh-Lot's presence prodding at the edge of his consciousness with increasing force. The ritual was working. Soon the dark lord of nightmares would once again roam the Earth. He would rid the world of this zombie pestilence. Giovanni would once again be free to prey on mortals to assuage his god's hunger.

These zombies merrily chanted the invocation Giovanni had taught them, following the steps the sorcerer had marked on the ground. These fools had no idea they were summoning their own doom!

The chant reached its conclusion; the dancing stopped. The sky grew dark; and Yamesh-Lot appeared: a gigantic chaos of dark tendrils that sprang from the centre of the star defined by the torches. Yamesh-Lot towered over the zombie suburb, blending with the darkness of the sky. The god's power flooded Giovanni's mind, and the sorcerer laughed loudly.

Yamesh-Lot's thick, gooey substance fully materialized. He captured the gathered zombies, wrapping them in His dark tendrils, preparing to consume their essence and transform them into nightmare acolytes who would haunt humanity's dreams in His name.

And then the zombies started to eat Giovanni's god. They chomped ravenously on the tendrils; they chewed and swallowed the black god meat like it was the best meal they'd ever had.

Giovanni felt his god's pain sear through him. The sorcerer screamed and fell on the ground writhing.

Berserk with feeding rage, the zombies ate through Yamesh-Lot's body with relentless ferocity.

Giovanni felt his god's presence fade. The ancient sorcerer—still ensconced within Basil—fainted, and then finally died, along with his god.

Basil never did tell Judith that he'd been possessed by the spirit of a fleshie animal. It was just too embarrassing. He had witnessed everything Giovanni had done with his body, but had been unable to act.

He'd noticed that Judith hadn't been altogether displeased by Giovanni's behaviour, and he wasn't about to give her the satisfaction of knowing that it had been someone else who had been so romantic with her. He'd never hear the end of it.

After that weirdness at the wedding anniversary party, as far as Basil could tell, the animal who'd invaded his mind was gone for good. What a relief! And the guests had sure enjoyed that unexpected snack. On the other hand, his suave jet-black eyes had turned a dull brown, and whereas they had seemed impervious to rot before, he felt them start to go mushy on him. He sighed. More spending.

No more black eyes for him, though. He'd get the cheapest eyes he could find next time; and he'd go alone. It had been Judith who'd insisted on the black eyes. That woman and all her ideas!

The funny thing, though, was that, a few hours after the party, Judith's eyes turned black. As did the eyes of all their guests.

The next day, Judith complained about bad dreams in which fleshies hunted her down, burned her body, and dropped the ashes into a dark pit, while gigantic black eyes looked down from the sky.

Judith gouged out her eyes, but they grew back.

ROMAN PREDATOR'S
CHIMERIC ODYSSEY

Already, dusk encroaches on daylight, and Luna, lushly green, hangs in the sky, its fullness announcing the hunt. Roman's mouth waters at the thought of fresh meat. It rained on the night of the last full moon, and the one before that; the monthly hunt is taboo on such occasions. Now, the only clouds are thin and wispy. It will not rain tonight. It must not. Roman does not want to be denied again.

Exhaling pungent smoke, he passes the joint to the smiling teenage girl next to him—he forgets her name—and gets up from the grass at the foot of Mount Royal. Nearby, bare-chested young men play tam-tams, girls dancing around them, shedding their clothes.

Roman has had enough of being around people. He

runs, first to the beat of the music, then gradually finds his own rhythm.

He runs up the mountain. He runs along well-worn paths, avoiding the tangle of branches, so he can go fast, faster, faster. He hopes to lose his nervous edge in the adrenaline rush. But the exertion has the opposite effect. His body yearns for the hunt.

Roman is worried that he might not be chosen as the Wolf's avatar tonight. He has been leading the hunt for the past five years, and he's been hunting for more than ten. That's longer than most hunters last. Soon, he knows, the Bishop will choose another to incarnate the Wolf, and Roman's hunting days will be over. As former pack leader, he would not submit to his replacement. Better to retire. The priests know this, and they wouldn't call on him to join another's pack.

He reaches the familiar lookout; some of the ancient concrete still peeks through the groundcover. The city stretches below him, stopping at the Wall, the centuries-old structure that keeps Montreal safe from the wild beasts and uncivilized peoples who inhabit the rest of the island. Once, the city was the whole island. Now the Wall defines the city's limits.

A loud cracking thunders from the sky. Roman turns his head toward the noise, cursing this unexpected turn in the weather. But there's no sign of rain. In the darkening but clear sky, something streaks groundward. Before he can contemplate this occurrence further, the church bells ring. Finally. Roman follows the path westward, up the mountain and down again, to the Oratory.

Night has fallen. The sixty hunters have gathered—unclothed, ready to receive the Wolf, should they be called.

There are two new faces: Lyana and Paul, replacing Phil and Van. Van, barely old enough to be called a man, was killed by a chimera in the previous hunt, his first outing; Phil, an experienced hunter, died not in the hunt but in his bed, after weeks spent coughing blood.

Lyana and Paul will hunt tonight. New graduates are always chosen. Kill or be killed, a harsh lesson all hunters learn quickly. Tonight, for the first time, the youths will be called by their full names.

Naked save for giant Wolf masks that cover not only their faces but also their chests, twelve acolytes pound the hunting drums. Roman's heart thumps in step. Behind him, unmasked acolytes in black robes tend the bonfires. Beyond the flames, behind the gates, on the streets and on the roofs of nearby buildings, people watch the ritual.

Twelve Wolf-masked priests clad in layers of wolf furs walk down the steps, their masks narrow but tall, extending a full metre above their shoulders. The priests carry goblets decorated with Wolf effigies. Each priest walks to a drummer, then turns toward the assembled hunters, holding a goblet as if in offering.

The drumming slows but gets louder. The Bishop emerges from atop the long, high staircase. She holds a leash; on the end of the leash is a muzzled wolf. A sacred beast engineered by priests versed in the arts of transmogrification of the flesh.

OBJECTS OF WORSHIP

The Bishop is naked. She is more than two metres tall, a monument of both fat and muscle. Her limbs are twice the girth of an average man's. Her ample thighs give way to massive hips. Her floppy breasts are held up by her belly, which spreads outward in every direction. Her neck disappears into the bloated globe of her face. She is completely hairless, from head to toe. Her light-brown skin is decorated with phosphorescent tattoos of the Wolf. She walks forward, holding the leash tight, and the wolf must step forward lest it be crushed by her bulk. The drums match her steps. She stops halfway down the long staircase. The drums grow quieter; they become nearly imperceptible, a subliminal collective heartbeat.

The first priest calls Paul Wayfinder; the second, Lyana Bloodmouth. Ten others are called. The chosen hunters each walk to their priest. In a solemn choreography, the hunters pull viscous knives from the goblets before them. Holding their left hands over the receptacles, they slice their palms, letting the blood drip into the goblets, into which they then dip their wounded hands. The drums sound one almost deafening boom and then stop. The hunters pull out their hands and stretch their healed palms toward the crowd.

There are forty-eight remaining hunters, many of them with young and strong bodies—good choices to welcome the Wolf. Roman, convinced he will not be called, can almost taste his disappointment.

In the silence, the Bishop's deep voice shouts a name: "Roman Predator."

Roman almost swoons as the anticipatory tension seeps

out of his body. But the newly resumed beat of the drums gets his heart beating, his blood flowing.

The unchosen hunters retreat to the edge of the Oratory grounds.

Holding raw, juicy ground meat in her hands, a naked, shaven, unadorned acolyte emerges from behind the Bishop. The acolyte, almost breastless, no more than thirteen years old, is comically petite next to the massive Bishop. But Roman does not laugh. He positions himself facing the Oratory's staircase, three metres from its foot.

The acolyte kneels in front of the muzzled wolf and pushes the meat in its face.

The wolf snarls and thrashes, tries to break free, but the Bishop keeps a tight, powerful hold on the leash.

Still holding the meat, the acolyte steps backward, turns, and continues down the stairs, each step echoed by the drums. The girl stops once she reaches Roman. Even without the Wolf in him, Roman can smell her. Her young, oiled skin. But Roman keeps his eyes fixed on the wolf.

The young acolyte smears the meat on Roman's naked body, lingering on the neck, the chest, the belly, the crotch.

The wolf stares back at Roman, pulling at the leash.

The acolyte stands up and pushes her meat-covered fingers into Roman's mouth. He licks them clean.

Amidst a flurry of chaotic drum beats, she runs back up the stairs, vanishing behind the Bishop.

The Bishop unleashes the wolf. The drummers intensify the furious beat. The muzzle falls from the animal's face, and it races down the steps toward Roman.

To prove his worth as pack leader, to incarnate the Wolf, Roman must kill the sacred beast. He has never failed this test.

Roman waits until the wolf is less than a metre from him. Then, just as the wolf's jaws are about to close on his stomach, the hunter somersaults above the beast, flipping around in mid-air. Stomach-first, Roman lands on the wolf's back, grabs the animal's head, crushes its eyes with his thumbs, then begins to twist its neck. But, for the first time in the five years Roman has been called to be the avatar, the ritual wolf shakes him off.

The blinded animal lunges toward Roman, its open mouth reaching for his crotch. He rolls away—barely in time. As the wolf's jaws snap shut, its teeth tear a strip of flesh from Roman's thigh.

Never before has a ritual wolf drawn Roman's blood. Rage fills the hunter. He kicks the wolf in the throat and jumps up to grab it from the back. This time, he gets a good grip on the head and succeeds in breaking the animal's neck.

Roman snarls in anger, conscious that such a poor performance, no matter how well the hunt itself goes, will result in tonight being his last time.

Roman rolls the dead animal onto its back. With his bare hands, he rips the animal open and feasts on its innards.

He pushes his forearm inside the still-warm corpse and clenches his fist around the beast's heart. He rips it out.

Roman raises his bloody face from the corpse and stands

up. Facing the Bishop, he bites into the wolf's heart. The twelve other hunters walk over to him. One by one, they take a bite out of the heart and offer Roman their goblets, with their blood mixed with the sacred ambrosia. With these potions, he washes down the wolf's blood.

The blood of the wolf, the blood of the hunters, and the ambrosia warm Roman's insides. He feels the liquids course within him, connecting him with his pack, changing him. His body expands, grows, becomes a receptacle for the Wolf. Fur grows on the hunter's body. His teeth sharpen. His nails take on the shape and strength of claws. His senses become more acute. An urgent need to feed, to kill, takes hold of his mind.

The others are changed, too, but their transformations are subtle. A heightening of the senses, perhaps meagre patches of fur here or there, a slight burst of growth, a thickening of their nails.

Roman issues a mental command to his pack. They follow him, daggers in hand, eager to kill. The cheering crowd parts before them.

Beyond the Wall, savage chimeras roam the island. They are descended from laboratory-created hybrids of the now extinct pre-BioWar megafauna. Tonight, Roman and his pack hunt chimeras.

The pack has felled three dozen beasts so far, including one giant, their latest kill. The giant—its head stood more than six metres off the ground, its body twelve metres long—had thick, orange-furred legs, two metres high;

a large horned and tusked head crowned with an orange mane; and a grey pachyderm hide covering its back and sides. But, as Roman discovered, its belly was soft and vulnerable and conveniently high off the ground. While his pack distracted the monster, he jumped up onto the beast's underside and sank three sets of claws into it, holding on while it screamed and thrashed. He tore into its guts with his free hand. Two of his hunters plunged their knives into its neck, leaving large bloody gashes as they tore them back out. Roman climbed onto the weakening giant's back, sank his teeth into the soft flesh of its neck, and ripped out its throat.

The other kills, although smaller beasts, no more than twice the size of a tall man, had been more dangerous prey. They'd all been fast, most of them feline in body shape and in movement. One of these had had three heads; another, an extra pair of limbs, arms that ended in six-clawed hands; yet another, a razor-sharp tail. Their first kill of the night had such powerful limbs that it could leap above their heads.

Now, Roman hunts alone as his pack brings their kills back to the city. Roman could end the hunt now. It's already been a good night, better than many hunts—and with no casualties to boot.

But the bloodlust won't let go of Roman. This is his last hunt; he will soon be forced to retire. Even if he is not replaced, perhaps the ritual wolf will kill him next time. He's not as young, as strong as he needs to be. Besides, once enough meat has been gathered for the community, it's the avatar's privilege to hunt alone, to feast on meat for the Wolf and no-one else. He catches a whiff of an unfamiliar smell. Blood, but not quite blood, or blood mixed with something... different. His curiosity aroused, he runs westward, toward the exotic scent.

The egg-shaped object must come from Luna, Roman thinks. *But . . . this is nothing like the rogue tech with which Luna occasionally infests the Earth. Perhaps,* he thinks with wonder, *this is something from beyond . . . something truly alien. A ship. A starship. An egg from space.*

The object's smooth surface cannot settle on any colour; seeing it—looking at it—requires concentration, as if it were only reluctantly visible.

It landed on a titanesque chimera, a lumbering behemoth with neither the speed nor the wits to avoid the fatal collision. The beast's head is submerged in the water, its body—what's left of it—splattered on the shore. It must have been drinking.

The egg—roughly Roman's size—is cracked open. As Roman approaches, he notices there are tentacles sprouting from within. Like the ship itself, they, too, shimmer at the edge of visibility, neither shape nor colour at all stable.

Roman trudges through the gore, getting closer to the ship.

The tentacles penetrate the chimera's corpse—no, they are merging with the beast. Even the egg itself is now losing definition, blending with the strewn bones and viscera of the animal. When the dead beast's head raises from the water and bellows, Roman is so startled that his feet slip on something viscous and he falls into the pulsing, slithering remains of the chimera. The animal has acquired a strange, disturbing afterlife.

Roman springs up. Instinctively, he bares his fangs and raises his claws. He rushes toward the egg and tears away a fistful of tentacles. Black blood spurts from the wounds, splattering everything. Roman licks his lips and tastes the dark blood. Immediately the Wolf rises from deep within him, and he feels his body expand again.

Roman bites into the tentacles in his hand, savouring the alien meat. He rips out more tentacles, tears their flesh with his fangs, feels the meat slide down his throat. The overflow of ichor clots the fur around his mouth.

Peering inside the open cavity of the vessel, he sees the creature within, a pulsing orb the size of a fat child, new tentacles shooting out of it to replace those Roman has eaten. Roman's jaws clamp down on the creature, and an agonized shriek issues from the mouth of the partially reanimated chimera. The chimera's head once more falls into the water. The impact causes a wave of water to splash over Roman. Momentarily startled, he pauses and looks at the creature in the egg. Inside the torn flesh, Roman cannot identify any organs or bones, only a mess of tightly constricted ligaments. The outer flesh of the creature is not distinct from its ovoid casing but rather like an inner membrane; the egg ship and the tentacled orb are either symbiotically merged or two parts of a single creature.

The Wolf overwhelms Roman, interrupting his thoughts.

He attacks. He feasts on the bizarre creature, devouring the orb, tentacles . . . devouring everything.

As first-time hunters it is Lyana and Paul's duty and privilege to attend to the physical needs of the avatar after the hunt. By now, as dawn breaks, all traces of the Wolf have vanished from the two youths. Roman—almost twice as tall as his normal size—admires their taut, naked young bodies. Paul's clean-shaven jawline is strong, his lips full. Lyana's ears are delicate, her shoulders broad.

Using fresh towels, they dry Roman's clean fur. It's unusual for the Wolf to linger so long and so strongly. But Roman enjoys it, delights in the strength and power.

While Lyana feeds the fireplace with more wood, Paul licks Roman's fangs. Lyana joins them and wraps her legs around one of Roman's massive thighs, rubbing herself. Roman feels her juices moistening his fur.

When Roman's consciousness is restored, there is no sign of either Lyana or Paul. The fire is out, and Roman can smell the juices of sex on his fur. The youths should have cleaned him. It was their duty and their privilege.

He stands up. His rooms appear unusually small to him. Roman's body has not yet reassumed its unaltered form.

Roman ventures outside. The sun tells him it's mid-morning. Instantly he feels eyes upon him. He smells fear. Whispers nag at his ears. People avoid him, but they stare furtively. The Wolf should have left him by now.

Roman breaks into a run. Running helps him think. Not this time, though. In a mounting panic, until sundown and beyond, he runs through the streets of Montreal. People stay out of his way. He smells fear wherever he goes.

As dawn breaks he rushes up the mountain, escapes into the trees, and collapses from exhaustion.

In the woods, Roman dreams of the past. But not of his past. Images, sounds, and scenes flash chaotically through his mind, blending into each other.

He feels himself lumbering through the brush, feeding on leaves and bark, fighting off predatory chimeras. Until something smashes into him, breaking his back. He remembers floating in a vast amniotic ocean, surrounded by others like himself, other shimmering blobs. Sometimes they float near each other, even touch each other. The contact is both painful and pleasurable. But then shells grow around the other blobs. A shell grows around him, isolating him. Still, the warmth of the amniotic ocean caresses his outer shell. There is turbulence. The warmth goes away and is replaced by an intense cold. And then he recognizes Montreal. Running in the streets and alleys. Playing with other children. Which one is he? He can't be sure. He spreads his shit on the wall and someone shouts at him: "Lyana!" For the first time, he touches the wetness between his legs, pushes a finger inside, and he gasps. He sees himself—no, sees Lyana—through someone else's eyes. She is under him, his weight presses down on her. Her fingernails digging into his back, she cries, "Paul . . ."

Then he sees himself—Roman—in his Wolf form. In his living room. He perceives himself from two perspectives at once: from Paul's and Lyana's. They are worshipping the Wolf, sharing pleasure with its avatar. Tendrils erupt from within Roman. The tendrils encircle the hunters' throats before they can scream. Roman's body shimmers, and the tendrils pull the youths into him, subsuming their bodies into his.

Roman wakes. He is attached to the ground by a mass of pulsing tendrils. Damp, decaying smells clog his mind. The sound of millions of scurrying feet echoes inside his head. He imagines himself deep in the soil, burrowing through the Earth. Screaming, he rips the tendrils from himself, where they grow out of his chest and belly and crotch. Viscous black goo oozes all over his fur. But the wounds close up quickly. The detached tendrils wither.

He looks up in the sky: Luna is once again full, lushly green. It's time to hunt.

Outside the grounds of the Oratory, the crowd parts before Roman. The people are so tiny. Like children—no, like infants. There are screams.

He walks through the gate and stands among the gathered hunters. He smells their fear. It angers him. The minuscule hunters do not flee, neither do they attack. They, too, part before him, letting him through. Roman ignores them.

At the foot of the stairs Tamara Meatfinder has killed the ritual wolf. She is ready to be the new avatar. But the

Wolf is still with Roman. There can be but one avatar, one pack leader. Must he kill her to retain his claim?

In an awed tone, the Bishop says, "Roman Predator?" The sound of his name rouses something within Roman, and he becomes aware of his strangeness, his wrongness.

All around him, the hunters and priests and acolytes whisper his name. Tamara shouts: "Roman the Wolf!" And a few of them fall to their knees, arms outstretched toward him in supplication. Then they all do it, repeating the exclamation—all except the Bishop.

Roman's skin itches, subtly ripples beneath the fur. His body aches to release tendrils, to gather all these bodies into his. Roman fights the impulse. What has he become? The priests can help him. They hold the secrets of transmogrification. They can restore him, maybe even extract Paul and Lyana, extract the . . . alien. This thing from beyond that is consuming him from the inside.

The Bishop walks down the stairs, toward Roman. He remembers her as this massive, imposing figure, and yet here she is at his feet, her head barely reaching his hips.

He sinks to his knees before her. He growls, "Help me."

She reaches out to touch him, strokes the fur of his belly. "How . . . ?"

The physical contact makes him lose control of his body. Tendrils wrap around the fat, muscular woman. She struggles, but it's over in an instant. She has been pulled into Roman's body, has dissolved into him.

Roman screams in rage and exasperation. The hunters and priests and acolytes cower. Roman runs away. Runs out the gate. Runs toward the Wall. Jumps over the Wall. Jumps so high it feels like flying. Escapes into the wilderness. Among the chimeras.

Roman Predator preys on chimeras. When the Wolf is strongest, he hunts them and eats them. When the alien ascends, he subsumes them.

The memories of so many creatures swirl in Roman's mind. He suspects he spends entire days, maybe even months or years, with other personalities dominating his hybrid, chimeric body. Sometimes, his consciousness regains control while he's in the middle of hunting, or feasting, or swimming, or praying. Or he finds himself in unfamiliar surroundings, his tendrils buried in the ground, or in a giant rock, or in a tree. Whenever his consciousness floats back to the surface, dreamlike shadow images swiftly parade through his mind's eye, but they vanish before they can leave an imprint on his memory.

Roman stumbles on a pack of nomadic savages. There are a few dozen of them—men, women, children, babies. Some of them have guns. He feels the bullets penetrate his skin. They sting, like bees.

The Wolf and the alien rise in tandem. Roman bares his fangs while a dozen tendrils sprout from his torso.

The savages scream and flee.

Roman pursues them. More bullets sting him.

Tendrils wrap themselves around the fleeing savages, pulling them in. Roman barely pauses as these new people merge with his chimeric body.

Within minutes it is over. Roughly half of the savages are now part of Roman. The Wolf slew the others.

He sniffs the freshly dead meat, then eats the rest of the pack.

The Bishop talks to him now. Together, they meditate and can control the body. Gradually, they integrate into a complex whole the various minds that inhabit it. The Wolf. The chimeras. The savages. They discover other sparks of awareness: insects, worms, arachnids, bacteria, trees, plants, fungus, rocks . . .

Finally, there is only the alien left to integrate. The hybrid mind attempts the contact. Communion is achieved. The last spark of Roman's individuality dissolves into this new, engulfing vastness.

The Roman Chimera swims down to the ocean floor. On the way, tendrils ensnare fish, immediately integrating them into its hybrid consciousness. Hordes of plankton penetrate the permeable flesh of the Roman Chimera, joining it. It feels the mounting pressure of the water on its skin, but the body adapts instantly to its environment.

When the Roman Chimera reaches the bottom, it creates a hard shell around itself. And then it drills down, downward into the Earth, through every layer, to the planet's core.

Having reached its destination, the Roman Chimera lets itself be subsumed. It feeds the Earth.

From the Earth's core, millions of microscopically thin tendrils erupt outward.

DESTROYER OF WORLDS

A woman—from my greying perspective almost a girl, really—took off her clothes and folded them in a neat pile at her feet. When she was done, she stood still, looking out toward the ocean. Nestled as I was among some large rocks in a shady nook of the beach, she couldn't have known I was there. I wasn't going to shatter her solitude by bringing attention to myself.

From where I sat the young woman was in profile. She had long strawberry-blond hair and a slim body, the kind you see on magazine covers. Her cheeks were covered with freckles, and her nose was turned in a peculiar way. I'd be lying if I said I didn't notice her full breasts, still firm enough to defy gravity.

But what struck me most, so much so that I felt a painful

twinge in my chest, was the resigned loneliness broadcast by her posture.

I had no idea who she was. I didn't know everyone in Singleton by name, but I rarely came across an unfamiliar face, especially at six in the morning.

She stepped into the ocean.

There was an oily, chemical stench in the air, coming in from the sea. She couldn't have been going for a swim. People knew better than to get in the water for pleasure anymore.

There was a deliberateness, a weight, to her gait. She was walking to her death.

I'm not one to interfere in other people's lives. Someone wants to kill themselves, it's their business and only their own. Suicide isn't a decision taken lightly. If someone does it at a time and place in which they have a right to believe that no-one will see them, then it's clearly not a cry for attention. It's a personal choice. You interfere with that—you try to "save" that person—and they'll have to go through that whole process of deciding to kill themselves. Again. That's cruel.

So that beautiful young woman—whoever she was—vanished beneath the waves.

Already, the tide nipped at her abandoned clothes, the wind scattering them.

Ten years ago, I sold my fishing license to a goddamned corporation when fishing licenses were still worth a mint. Paid off what little was left on my mortgage. Was able to retire at forty-five. Janet kept her job at the bank, even though I told her she didn't have to. But she liked to get out of the house, and most of her friends worked there. The extra money was nice, but at first her decision left me lonely. We had gotten married when we were twenty-five, but we had never really spent enough time together and I was hoping early retirement would change all that. That we'd get to enjoy each other again while we were still young enough.

It took me about a year to come to terms with the fact that Janet and I would never get any closer. We were reliable, loving companions, but we would never burn up the world with romance and passion. I accepted this quietly, never mentioning it to her. She was concerned about my indolence, worried that it might turn into depression. Gradually, the mood passed.

I'd never wanted to become a fisherman. My dad and his brothers had all been fishermen. So had my granddad. I didn't envy their lives. In fact, when I was young, I hated it. I yearned to escape this town and the life my folks had brought me into. I used to dream about being an artist, a writer, an archaeologist—anything that would take me away from Singleton. I filled up notebook after notebook with comics stories of the impossibly glamorous adventures I would enjoy if I ever escaped this place. I loved drawing monsters and girls best of all.

I tried to emulate the work of my favourite cartoonist, Jake Kurtz. His stuff exploded with energy. His panels were framed in odd, disorienting angles. He filled up his pages with intricate designs and vividly imagined settings of strange worlds. I desperately needed life to be as exciting and wondrous as his comics.

On my sixteenth birthday, Dad had a stroke that left his left side partially paralyzed. He needed me on the boat after that. There wasn't enough money for any other option. The night before my first day out, I silently cried myself to sleep.

I'd been out with my dad often as a little kid, so I knew my way around the boat, more than I cared to admit. I didn't expect to be good at it, much less to like it.

But I was surprised at how much I did end up enjoying it. Dad died of another stroke about six years later. During the intervening years we became friends, something I had never believed possible. I wish he could have been around for my wedding. He hated dressing up, and we would have shared a good laugh about it.

People in Singleton saw me as a traitor for selling my license. Back then I could tell that not only were the fish dying off but more and more of the catch was contaminated. I got out while the going was still good. I didn't hurt anyone. The situation with the ocean was way past the point of no return. We were all responsible for the damage we'd done to the sea and to the fish. No use fighting a war that had already been lost. Still, I didn't exactly have any friends around here anymore. Even ten years later—as if it was my fault that the fish died out and the ocean was a poisonous cesspool. Hell, humanity as a group was destroying the whole world, species by species, ecosystem by ecosystem.

Selling my license didn't precipitate that.

I tried to talk Janet into moving away, but she'd lived here her whole life and didn't want to leave behind everyone and everything she knew.

I sat there for about an hour after the young woman disappeared into the ocean, numbed. I knew I'd done the right thing by not interfering, but it was a hell of a thing to witness. And seeing something so obviously intended to be a private moment felt dirty and invasive.

I got up. The sun hit my eyes. The cloudless summer sky was a bright, almost glowing blue. I made my way back home barely in time to fix breakfast before Janet had to leave for work. I didn't mention the woman to Janet—because I didn't really know what to say about it, but also because it would have impinged even more on that woman's privacy. It was her death, not anyone else's, and I didn't have the right to take it away from her.

As we did every morning, Janet and I ate breakfast quietly. Janet isn't really awake until she's halfway through her second cup of coffee. Before that she doesn't do much more than grunt. By the time she left, the skies weren't so clear anymore. Dark grey clouds formed over Singleton, and the wind carried a hint of fierceness. Now that I was alone, the weird morning suddenly caught up with me. I was anxious, fidgety, filled with tumultuous emotions that mirrored the sudden storm.

I should have been doing housework, but I couldn't focus. I sank into my reading chair, listening to the rush of the wind outside.

The doorbell rang a few minutes later. It was Donald Hodge, the UPS driver. He made a comment about the unexpected turn in the weather—there wasn't even a speck of blue sky anymore, and the wind was gaining strength by the minute. I signed for my parcel: a box from The Golden Age comics shop. Even the barely concealed contempt that hid behind Donald's superficial cordiality—that underlying disdain that too many people in Singleton held for me—couldn't spoil my excitement. This treasure was what I needed to shake off the day's unsettling oddness.

I opened the box, knowing already what was inside: *Greatest Comics* #3–13—the never-reprinted complete run of Jake Kurtz's "The Preservers," before the strip graduated to a comic book of its own. Kurtz and Shrugging Atlas Comics never did work out their legal wrangles over those episodes: Kurtz owned the stories, but the publisher owned the characters. As a result, the original Preservers stories were never seen again.

I had copies of nearly everything else Kurtz had ever worked on, in addition to a complete set of the post-Kurtz version of *The Preservers* comic book. This run of *Greatest Comics* came out a few years before I started reading comic books, so I missed them the first time around and had never found copies I could afford. These were in poor condition, but at least I could finally read the stories.

For years Kurtz continued to work for smaller publishers, writing and drawing all his stories, until his death in 1994. His oeuvre encompassed every genre imaginable, westerns, romance, humour, superheroes, fantasy, war . . . and, what many consider his specialty, monster stories. His most admired work was a 250-page mythological epic called *Destroyer of Worlds*, from the mid-1970s. His comics were always praised by connoisseurs, but sales didn't match the critical acclaim.

The Preservers were Stanley King, the patriarch of his family, a shapeshifter who called himself Professor Unknown; his wife, Suzanne, who could become intangible and who adopted the name Spectral; their daughter, Sandy, a.k.a. the Human Angel, who sprouted wings that gave her the ability to fly; and Stanley's younger brother, Cliff, who was transformed into a superstrong ten-foot, blue-scaled giant called the Brute. They gained their powers when, after their private jet crashed in the Himalayas, they were rescued by the god Vishnu, the preserver, who granted them strange abilities "to preserve the world against the forces of destruction."

Something hard thudded against the house, and that jarred me out of Kurtz's universe. I looked out the window. Although it was only around noon, it was as dark as dusk. Trees were bending dangerously against the wind. The rain was still sparse, but it was obvious it would soon be torrential.

I switched on the TV. The weather channel was issuing a severe storm warning, urging everyone to stay indoors. The announcer emphasized that winds were now expected to reach hurricane strength.

OBJECTS OF WORSHIP

I was concerned about Janet. I wanted to be sure she wouldn't try to leave work in the middle of this mess. Best that she stay there until it was all over. I tried to call her, but the phone was dead. I needed to hear her voice, to reassure myself. I calmed down by reminding myself that Janet was much too reasonable to do something as careless as going outside in this kind of weather.

Through the window, I saw the wind uproot the tree on the Irvings' lawn across the road. I grabbed my pile of *Greatest Comics* and ran to the cellar.

Even down there, I heard the storm rage. Stuck in the cellar, I eagerly plunged into my new, long sought-after acquisitions—but the electricity went out. In the dark, I fumbled around for the shelf where we kept emergency supplies. I found the flashlight, and I also lit some candles.

Willing myself to be oblivious to the sounds of the destructive weather, I returned to the welcome escape of Kurtz's imagination.

"The Preservers," as originally conceived by Jake Kurtz, was different in tone and content than the version later published by Shrugging Atlas Comics. Kurtz's characters weren't so much superheroes, as they became under other hands, but explorers. The mythological nature of their origins and powers was played up more heavily, and the stories concerned themselves with hidden societies, old gods, and magical artefacts rather than supervillains and the like. Themes and ideas later explored in *Destroyer of*

Worlds—such as humans being pawns in complex games and conflicts between the gods of various pantheons— were first hinted at in these stories.

The most shocking episode of Kurtz's "The Preservers" was the last one: "The Mysterious Suicide." Professor Unknown sees a sobbing woman on a secluded beach walk into the ocean. Despite his efforts, he fails to prevent it, and her body vanishes under the water. Soon after the suicide— while King is still trying to locate the body—a savage storm erupts. It hits the nearby town. The Preservers use their powers to protect the townspeople from the storm. As the weather calms, Professor Unknown spots the woman from the beach driving away. Alive.

The story ended there, the final panel being a blurb for the never-published follow-up episode: "Next! The Hunter Strikes!"

When silence fell, its starkness was almost deafening.

I had by then reread "The Mysterious Suicide" several times, trying in vain to make sense of its similarity to my own experiences.

What I found when I emerged from the cellar helped me focus on something other than a comics story written and drawn half a century ago.

All our house's windows had been shattered. Stupid old man. Too focused on my comics, I'd forgotten the storm shutters; I should have gone out and secured them as soon as the weather showed signs of turning foul. There were shards of glass, rocks of various sizes, and all kinds of debris littering the floor and the furniture. The pictures that had hung on the walls—all of them Janet's: family photos, works by local artists, a painting of her as a baby by her long-dead father—had fallen, the frames broken. It was going to take a lot of work and expense to fix all this.

I tried calling Janet again, but the phone lines were still down.

I should have stayed and cleaned up the damage. But it was too much, too extensive. I couldn't face it. I left the house, rushing to join Janet at the bank. To make sure she was okay.

Singleton looked like a war zone.

Oily blotches, presumably from the ocean, splattered all over. Cars smashed up and turned upside down. Debris, shattered to unidentifiable fragments, strewn everywhere. Dead birds and squirrels on the ground, limbs and heads ripped off. Even some fish and seaweed lying here and there. House walls wrecked by uprooted trees. Our home hadn't fared that badly, all things considered.

The closer I got to Main Street, the more panicked and wounded people I encountered. Ambulances, police cars, and military trucks were already on the scene, with personnel doing what they could to help. The enormity of the destruction was too much to grasp.

On our way back from the bank, Janet and I kept stopping to talk to townsfolk: old man Steinberg from the post office, the Bradfords (who both used to work for me back in the day), Taylor from the hardware store . . . They were all unusually friendly, as if we were good neighbours, as if the last decade had never happened. Part of me wanted to stay resentful, but I let it go.

Everywhere people chatted, helping each other out, and making plans to work together to rebuild the town. Amidst all this destruction, Singleton felt like a community again. Like a community I was a part of. I wasn't naive enough to believe that people liked me again, but, in the wake of the storm, disliking me stopped being so important. It was a start.

As we walked home, Janet held my hand with a firmness I hadn't felt since the first months of our marriage.

Next to me, Janet slept. I kissed her shoulder, eliciting a drowsy moan, and then I slipped out of bed. I got dressed, wandered through our wrecked home, and, restless, went out for a midnight walk.

I didn't have a destination in mind, but I wasn't surprised when I realized I was heading toward the ocean. What did surprise me was the shiny, expensive-looking black car with tinted windows parked near the path in the woodsy area that led down to the secluded beach. Nobody in Singleton had a car like that. I approached it and peered into the windows, but they were too opaque. I didn't want to touch the vehicle; it might have a sensitive alarm.

Stealthily, I made my way down to the beach. There was a man standing there, facing the ocean, away from me. He was very tall—well above six feet—and wore blue jeans and a brown turtleneck. He was pointing some kind of hand-held device toward the water; it emitted a high-pitched *ping!* as he arced slowly from east to west and back again. He repeated the gesture several times before folding up the machine.

As he turned around, I quickly dropped to the ground and tried, as silently as possible, to hide in the foliage.

When he reached the path, he stopped. I saw him take out his device again. He pointed it at the woods on both sides of the path. The *ping!* sound was especially grating from this close. I stifled a gasp when I got a closer look at the device. It resembled exactly those impossibly intricate Jake Kurtz machines from *Destroyer of Worlds*, with mazes of exposed circuitry arranged like some kind of alien alphabet.

The man folded the device again and walked up the rest of the path. The next few minutes dragged on, but eventually I heard the roar of a car engine. When I reached the main road, the black car was gone.

I took the path back down to the beach and sat in the wet sand staring at the ocean until sunrise, bewildered yet oddly excited. I was about to head back home when the woman walked out of the water and onto the beach.

In the aftermath of the storm, the morning air was unseasonably chilly. She was naked, just as she'd been when I'd last seen her yesterday. But she seemed untroubled by the cold.

When she saw me, panic briefly seized her features. She made no attempt to cover herself.

I waved hello, trying to seem as unthreatening as possible.

She hesitated, but then she walked up and sat next to me. I silently offered her my jacket. She declined, but I insisted. It was more for me, anyway. She nodded, but we still hadn't exchanged a word.

I tried small talk, but after a few awkward unfinished sentences that provoked no reaction from her, I decided— what the hell—to launch right into it even if it did sound crazy.

"Okay. The way I figure it, you're not really human. At least not normal human. Maybe even alien. There's some people hunting you—maybe others like you, maybe government—and you hid in the ocean for a whole day. That's either as long as you could stand or maybe you somehow figured they'd lost the trail. I don't know what kind of senses or powers or whatever you have. And you've done this before, hiding in the ocean. Maybe I should be scared of you. But I'm not."

She tentatively smiled at me. "You're not far from the truth."

I waited.

She wasn't saying anything else, so I told her how I had seen a tall man pointing a strange device at the ocean. I looked at her closely while I related that, and I saw her tense up.

She let out a deep breath, turned toward me, and said, "I was fortunate. Fossil-fuel residue can confuse the scanner, and the water here reeks of it."

"He tried the scanner on me. In the woods. And it didn't work."

"The device is calibrated to locate me. It doesn't register anyone else."

I waited again.

This time, she broke the silence. "Where am I?"

I hadn't expected that. "I'm not sure what you mean."

"I mean, tell me about this place. The city, the country, the government, the date. The rest of the world. Everything."

She nodded at the things I told her, as if checking the facts against her memory.

More silence.

Then, "Did anything else unusual happen?"

I told her about the storm.

She nodded. "Yes, that always happens." But she didn't elaborate. Another mystery. She persisted, "No other strangers?"

I shook my head.

"That's good. They haven't reached this place yet." They? Before I could ask, she said, "Do you really want to help me?"

Her eyes smouldered with a ferocity at odds with her imploring tone. Her body language was so different from the previous day, when, resigned and defeated, she had walked into the ocean. She seemed like an entirely different person. For a second, I became afraid of her. But then I nodded. I was surprised at how sure I was of my answer.

I had glimpsed something else in her eyes. I couldn't articulate what it was—but it awakened a profound longing.

Janet was picking through the broken wall hangings. Casually, even half-cheerfully, she asked, "Where were you?"

We kissed hello. Her mouth was delicious. It had been years since she'd kissed me so playfully.

"Couldn't sleep. Went out and walked around. The dawn light makes the destruction look especially eerie."

I got a garbage bag from the kitchen and started sorting through the debris. We spent the whole day cleaning up. I couldn't remember the last time Janet and I had such a good time. The day whizzed by while we worked, joked around, and reminisced. I was falling in love again.

Despite all that, my thoughts kept straying to the strange young woman who had walked in and out of the ocean and to the man in the black car.

After supper, Janet—exhausted from a full day's work around the house and hit hard by postprandial wooziness—went upstairs to nap, and I took the opportunity to rummage through her old clothes to find something for the stranger. I also got her some food. I had offered to bring her home—although I was hesitant at the idea of sharing my knowledge of this woman's existence with anyone, even Janet—but the stranger insisted she could hide in the water or in the woods until she was ready to leave. All that mattered was that she keep safe and out of sight until "they" got here. Her story remained vague, but she skirted around direct questions. Like a liar. Or a crazy person.

When I returned to the beach, dusk was softening the summer brightness.

OBJECTS OF WORSHIP

I called out "Hello!" and the stranger emerged from the woods that isolated the beach from the town. Her eyes told me how furious she was, and the tone of her voice confirmed it. "Where were you?" Janet had asked me that same question, but the meaning was different this time.

I promised I'd come back later, probably even that very night. "I have to go back. Our house is still a wreck . . . and there's so much to do around town. I do want to stay, but I have other responsibilities."

We almost argued, but she managed to keep her temper from boiling.

On the way home, I considered not returning to the beach. The stranger's arrogance irritated me, but she intrigued me too much and I knew I'd be back the next day. In some way, despite the evidence of her walking, breathing, talking body, I still thought of her as dead, and, as the only witness to her "death," I felt responsible for her.

When I climbed into bed, Janet stirred. She mumbled a greeting while I kissed her nape. I settled in and spooned her. She fell asleep again immediately. I was exhausted, too, but I couldn't get the stranger out of my head. It was several hours before I finally succumbed to a sleep haunted by nightmares—the stranger and me running, wounded, hunted by giant monsters from Jake Kurtz's comics.

"Soon," she said, "they will come. Their technology allows them to locate my point of entry, but, unlike Hunter, they have no scanner to find me once they arrive."

Hunter. I managed to suppress my reaction. A mixture of fear, shock, and excitement. Kurtz's final episode of "The Preservers" had ended with the unfulfilled promise: "Next! The Hunter Strikes!"

"Hunter will detect their arrival. That's when I'll need you most. You must distract them. All of them. So I can . . ." Her voice trailed off. She looked into my eyes, as if to see how much she could trust me. It was cold that night, but it was also beautiful. Not a cloud in the dark sky, and the stars sharp, bright points. There was no wind, and I almost convinced myself that the ocean smelled like it used to when I was a teenager and we could swim in it.

For five days now, I'd been dividing my time between fixing up the house with Janet, renewing my bonds with the Singleton community, and keeping the stranger company on the beach.

At my every visit the stranger repeated her story, adding a detail or two with each retelling. "Hunter wants to kill me, regardless of the consequences. He enjoys my suffering. He'll take his time, he'll torture me—he always does. But they . . . they want to capture me. They're convinced I'm dangerous. They also believe I'm more of a threat dead than alive. They want to get to me before Hunter finds me. But I can't trust them; they've betrayed me before."

"Why don't you leave here, then? Flee to somewhere none of these people can find you?"

She didn't answer. Her attention turned inward, as if she'd forgotten I was there.

I waited a few minutes, my mind buzzing with questions

about this bizarre and possibly insane woman, and then I asked her another question, almost certain she wouldn't answer that one either. "You keep saying 'they'—who are you talking about?"

"A family of adventurers. The Kings."

I suddenly felt very dizzy. "The Preservers?"

The stranger rose and bared her teeth. "You know them!" She struck me on the side of the head, and it sent me sprawling on the sand.

"No, I don't!" Her fists were clenched, and her eyes spat her anger at me. What insanity had I let myself fall into? I spoke quickly, hoping to quell her fury. "They're not real! They're characters in comic books. A man called Jake Kurtz invented them."

She sat again, partially mollified but suspicion still clouding her eyes.

I asked her, "Who are you?"

"You really don't know, do you?" She frowned. "After . . . afterward, once I get what I need from them, once I can escape from all this . . . I'll tell you everything. If you still want to know." She was almost crying. "For now, I'm betting this life that they'll get here before Hunter returns."

The stranger was silent for a long time, her face flickering between sadness and fury. Then she asked me about Jake Kurtz and his connection to the Kings, so I told her about my obsession with comics, and with his work in particular. I stopped paying attention to her as I got excited describing Kurtz's early monster comics, and the Preservers, and *Destroyer of Worlds*. I never got to speak to anyone about this stuff, not even Janet, who only silently tolerated my comics habit.

The stranger's fingers grasped my arm in a tight vise as I detailed Shiva's devious schemes in *Destroyer of Worlds*. For the first time since I'd launched into my speech, I took a good look at her. She was pale, shivering, frightened.

Part of me was more convinced than ever that she was simply a crazy woman who imagined herself in the middle of some superhero story she'd once read. But that theory couldn't explain the man—Hunter, if that really was his name—with the pinging device.

Before I could say anything more, she said, "Leave me alone. Go back to your life."

I returned to the beach two mornings later, with fresh bread, scrambled eggs in a plastic container, and two thermoses, one filled with orange juice, the other with coffee. Noisily, to make sure the stranger knew I was there, I set myself up among the rocks where I'd first seen her walk into the water.

I drank coffee, hoping she was still here. Wishing she'd come out and talk to me. I was worried about her, and I wanted to know why she'd grown so scared the other night.

Within fifteen minutes, she joined me, emerging from the small woods. The dress she wore—a frilly, knee-length blue thing with a revealing, low-cut neckline—I remembered when Janet bought it, fifteen, maybe sixteen years ago. We'd taken a day off in the middle of summer and gone shopping at the new mall that had opened a couple of towns over. I'd picked that dress for her from a sale rack, and she loved it. Janet had grown a bit too plump for it eventually, and, besides, it had a few holes and tears now. Janet would never wear anything in such a state, even though she knew I found scruffy clothes sexy.

The stranger accepted breakfast wordlessly. When the eggs, bread, coffee, and juice were all gone, she said, "Thank you for coming back. And for befriending me. I've not had a friend in a long time."

I nodded mutely, not trusting myself to have the right words. I feared igniting her volatile temper again.

We sat together in silence, getting used to each other's presence.

After a while I recounted that dream in which the two of us were hunted by Jake Kurtz's absurd monsters.

The dream made her laugh. A new sound; a deep, unselfconscious, guffawing laughter. For the first time, I relaxed around her.

"Let me tell you a story," she said.

I spent the whole day listening to her stories of wondrous worlds—alternate realities where every fancy could be true. Where history had taken other paths. Where monsters roamed. Where the continents had formed in different configurations. Where alien species walked the Earth. Where gods and animals and humans crossbred into exotic new permutations. Where superbeings flew through the skies.

Worlds, she told me, that she had visited.

Janet played with her food and avoided my eyes. She was preparing to tell me something difficult. I knew it was best to let her get to it at her own pace.

I finished my lasagna, cleared my plate, and came back to sit next to her.

She put her fork down and said, "I've noticed food disappearing. Recent leftovers that neither of us ate. A whole unopened box of crackers. A bag of raisins. Other stuff, too. And you've gone through my clothes. One of my old dresses is missing."

She paused and looked at my face.

Tension knotted my back. I didn't know what to tell her, or even if she wanted me to respond.

"You sneak away for hours at a time. You get up in the middle of the night and don't come back until dawn. You think I don't notice, but I do."

All I had to do was tell her about the stranger. Janet wasn't paranoid or jealous. If I told her the truth—that I'd been helping a woman stranded by the storm—she'd believe me. But that wasn't the whole truth. Janet would want to help, too, and I couldn't face such an intrusion into the insular world of the beach. I didn't know how to explain myself without sounding crazy, or without exposing something that felt too private to share—even with Janet.

I didn't say anything.

Later that day, while Janet was running some errands, I packed my camping gear. I left a note, apologizing for not being able to share with her what was going on with me.

Apologizing for suddenly taking off. I didn't tell her where I was going. I didn't tell her why. The note said: *I hope you'll still be able to welcome me when I return.* I wrote that I loved her, and I meant it, even as I was probably destroying whatever affection she still felt for me.

I wouldn't have been able to leave if Janet had been there to talk me out of it. And I didn't want her to. I didn't.

I joined the stranger on the beach.

Together we waited for "them." For the Preservers.

I couldn't stop thinking about Janet, but otherwise I enjoyed being a beach bum. No-one ever came here, so Janet wouldn't find me. If she even bothered to try after what I did to her. Occasionally, I'd go into town and buy some food. Word had gotten around about how I'd abandoned my wife, and people were ruder to me than ever. The Johnsons barely tolerated my presence in their grocery store.

When all this was over, when the woman was safe—or at least when I'd done what I could to help her, or whatever it was I was doing—I'd go back to Janet. If she'd still have me.

Or maybe I'd become a lonely old grouch. Or I'd finally leave this dump of a town.

Most of my time on the beach was spent alone, while the stranger hid. I crooned old sailing songs to the seagulls.

The same thought kept nagging at me, no matter how hard I tried to let go of it: how unbelievably stupid it was to leave Janet just as the fun and the passion were finally coming back into our relationship. Or was all that just a temporary byproduct of the storm? Maybe it had been best not to hope it would last. Eventually, life would have returned to banal, numbing normality.

I spoke to the stranger about my life, about what she called "this world." She described more of the myriad worlds that she claimed to have visited. But she was tight-lipped about her personal details. And no matter how I prodded and asked, she wouldn't say how she had travelled to these countless alternate realities. "After," she kept reminding me, "I'll tell you everything."

I didn't know if I really believed the stranger. I both did and didn't, somewhat apprehensive of either possibility. I wanted to believe that the universe was as fantastic as her stories made it out to be.

But it was all so crazy. And yet . . . how had she spent an entire day under the water? And what about that man she called Hunter, with his Jake Kurtz technology?

Maybe she hadn't really spent that much time in the water . . . maybe she had surfaced somewhere and then swum back . . . and that man could be from a secret high-tech government agency or something.

She could be a crazy woman who needed help. Maybe I was projecting too much of my own imagination into all this. Was I really helping her by encouraging her delusions?

I was skipping rocks on the water when a violent burst of hot wind knocked me down. I looked up. They had arrived.

A woman in skin-tight dark leather, her scalp shaved to stubble and her face covered with tattoos and piercings. Large, feathery wings sprouted from her back. Sandy King was no longer a teenager, but a woman of . . . sixty? Sixty-five?

Another woman in a similar leather outfit: her trim body gave the illusion of youth, but her weathered face revealed her age. In the comics, no-one ages, but Suzanne King must have been at least eighty.

Cliff King's age was harder to tell. Ten feet tall, his entire body covered in blue scales, he looked only remotely human.

Stanley King, holding a metal pad that could have been designed by Jake Kurtz, looked twenty-five. But he could mold his features into any shape.

Behind them, a gaping portal into the unknown, a gateway to the fantastic world they had come from, still leaked a prodigious amount of heat.

I hadn't really believed her until this moment. Now I had no choice but to believe. I wept, partially from the blast of burning heat but also from joy that the universe truly was as wondrous as I'd dreamed as a boy.

The Human Angel. Spectral. The Brute. Professor Unknown. "The Preservers!"

Professor Unknown spoke. "You know who we are?"

I had to pretend to know less than I did. For her. But there was still so much I didn't know.

"The Preservers are my favourite comics characters. Is this a movie set or something? What kind of special effect is that thing . . . that hole behind you?"

"Comics? In this universe, we're characters in comic books? Interesting."

"Stanley," said Spectral. "There's no time for all that."

"You're right, Suzanne. Sir, I wish we had time to explain, but we really are the Preservers." As if to highlight the Professor's claims, the Human Angel spread her wings and flew up into the dawn sky.

I gasped in awe. Could I really deceive these people? I wiped my eyes dry. Already the heat from the portal was receding.

Stanley King addressed me again. "We're looking for someone. A woman."

Before I could respond, the Human Angel landed back among her family. She looked at me. "I saw a tent over there." She nodded toward it. "Do you live on this beach?"

I said that I did.

Professor Unknown asked me, "Has anything peculiar happened here recently?"

"You mean more peculiar than superpowered comics characters coming to life?" That came out more facetious than I'd intended.

Suzanne interrupted. "Sir, I'm afraid this is rather urgent. Your world is in danger. As are countless others, unless we capture this woman. So, if you don't know anything, we'll be on our way."

"No, wait. I think I know who you mean. But, if you ask me, she seems to be the one in trouble, not the world."

Professor Unknown said, "Please continue."

"Well, about a month ago, a young woman I'd never seen before walked into the ocean. No-one ever swims or anything here. The water's too contaminated. Anyone going into that water has only one thing in mind, and that's killing themselves. And then, that very day, there was a monstrous storm, the worst I've seen in my whole life. Tore the town apart."

I hesitated. Could I betray her to these heroes? She was in my care—whoever, whatever she was. There was a fragile loneliness that hid behind all that pent-up fury of hers, and that moved me. Impulsively, not fully in control of the fact that I was doing so, I made up a story, borrowing details from a chapter of Kurtz's *Destroyer of Worlds*.

"The next day, she walked out of the ocean, dressed in a silver metal bodysuit overlaid with the same kind of circuitry design as that pad you're holding—"

Interrupting me, Spectral murmured to herself, "How did she get a hold of that kind of technology?" She looked worried, but mostly impatient. "What happened next?"

"And at that moment a big guy ran out from that path over there and started shooting at her, firing a strange-looking gun, again with those circuitry markings. What is that stuff? I've never seen anything like it in my whole life."

"Please, it's important that we know where these people went," Professor Unknown replied, ignoring my question.

"I think you're going to have to tell me what this is all about before I say anything more. The girl was scared. That maniac was hunting her."

Sandy barked, "Listen, you filthy bum, there's no time for that. Tell us what you know."

The Brute gently put a hand on her shoulder, while Professor Unknown harrumphed.

Stanley said, "I apologize for that, sir; we've all been under tremendous stress." He cleared his throat again. "You were right, when you first saw that woman, she was in all likelihood committing suicide. And she succeeded. She died. Then the second time you saw her, someone else— something else—was inhabiting her body. What you saw emerge from the ocean was a reanimated corpse taken over by a destructive entity that lays waste to universes as she travels from timeline to timeline. We want to capture her and hold her until we can figure out how to neutralize her threat."

"If she's so dangerous, why not simply kill her?"

"Because her death is what triggers the travel between dimensions, and she can't leave a timeline without automatically destroying it. The entity's new avatar is always a freshly dead woman."

"And that maniac?"

"He's called Hunter. His homeworld was destroyed by a previous avatar of the entity. He's obsessed with vengeance. He tracks her down from world to world, killing her every time, regardless of the consequences."

"But . . . doesn't he die when the worlds get destroyed?"

"No. He automatically jumps to the avatar's next destination world, though not necessarily near her point of arrival. Sometimes it takes him months to track her down, sometimes hours. On many worlds, there's a network, a secret society devoted to his master, that awaits his arrival and helps him. He's only an agent of her true enemy, a much more powerful entity."

"Do these . . . entities . . . have names?"

"She is Kali, and her enemy is her husband, Shiva, the destroyer of worlds. It's all a game to them."

I gulped. Kali? The stranger was a Hindu goddess? The same Kali that Jake Kurtz had written about in *Destroyer of Worlds*? Could I trust her? Should I? These people—the Preservers—were heroes. They saved worlds. They didn't destroy them. At least, that's what the comic books said.

I continued lying to my heroes. "Then they both flew away. Like superheroes. Or like gods, I guess. And I never saw them again. I guess this 'Hunter' hasn't caught up to her, because the world's still here."

The Brute suddenly moved more quickly than could be expected of a creature of his size and girth. He knocked all of us to the ground, shielding us from a ray beam striking from the sky. He grunted in pain but appeared otherwise unhurt.

Sandy King snarled, "Hunter."

Our attacker flew with the aid of another Kurtz-like machine, a one-man platform with curved handle controls. Another beam shot from one of the handles.

The Human Angel flew straight at Hunter, evading his ray beams. The powerful Brute valiantly shrugged off direct hits from Hunter's weapon as if they were insect bites. Spectral became nearly invisible and rose into the air toward their foe. Professor Unknown shouted instructions at his family, coordinating their efforts.

While the Preservers and Hunter fought, I crawled into the woods. To relative safety.

Kali, or whoever she was, found me and enfolded me in her arms.

I was trembling, the surreality of the dangers around me taking its toll. Her lips brushing my ear, she whispered, "I have to leave now, while they're busy fighting Hunter. I can't fail again. This must end now."

I trembled even more.

Despite her stated urgency, she stayed put. She had never stood this close to me. Her arms around me, I felt her tremendous physical strength, and I nuzzled deeper into her embrace.

She said, "I heard everything. Thank you. It's good to finally have a friend."

She pressed her hand against my chest, helping me slow my breathing, calming me down.

She told me her version. "They have some of it right, but not all of it. Yes, I am Kali. Yes, my husband, Shiva, plays a game of cat-and-mouse with me, destroying worlds in the process, so that new worlds may be born. These Preservers mean well, but at least once before they have played into my husband's hands. This is beyond them. Vishnu overestimated their effectiveness."

"They're just pawns in these games of yours?"

Kali ignored my question. "I want to end this; their plan would only enable my husband's agent to find me more easily, to torture me at his leisure. They cannot seriously oppose Shiva, who has been playing these games for millennia. Years ago, I proposed to Stanley King that he give me one of his dimensional travel devices. According to the rules set by my husband, Hunter can only follow if he kills me, not if I travel by other means. But King feared that the world would be destroyed in my wake, regardless of how I left."

"Would it?"

"I don't know. Probably. Yes. But then, Hunter would die along with it, and perhaps I would live forever in the new world, and this game of destruction, perpetuated at my expense, might end. I know my husband—he must be bored by this sport by now and would not start it afresh by going to the trouble of finding a new pawn."

I wanted to believe her. To trust her. Maybe I did. Maybe I didn't. Maybe it didn't matter.

"What about Kurtz? What does he have to do with all this?"

"From what you say of him, he sounds like an aspect of Brahma, the creator."

"And the woman . . . this woman whose body you took over—who was she?"

"She killed herself. The details don't matter." Kali stood up. "I have to leave now. I can still tap into the portal's residual energy and travel between worlds, but I can tarry no longer."

Yet, she hesitated. She held out her hand. "Come with me. To a new world. To a new life."

I thought about how fed up I was of life in Singleton. I nursed old angers: the polluted oceans, and all the other ways we were destroying the world that gave us life.

But then I thought about all the people and animals

and cities on Earth. About all the suns and planets in the universe. About the Preservers, doomed to perish in this mundane world after decades of astonishing adventures. I thought about everything that Kali would soon destroy.

How could an entire universe be annihilated so casually?

I wept.

I remembered my wife. It felt like a lifetime since I'd last seen Janet. I was suddenly overwhelmed by the urge to hold her, to taste her. The smell of her skin came back to me, and my heart ached with desire to see her again.

But perhaps it was time for all of this to end. Quickly. Painlessly. For another world, perhaps a better world, to be born from this one's destruction.

Perhaps I was full of shit—justifying a monstrous offer I could not bring myself to refuse.

I took Kali's hand. While Hunter and the Preservers still battled, we raced for the unguarded portal and stepped into another world, a world only Jake Kurtz could have imagined.

THIS IS THE ICE AGE

Distorted cars litter the bridge, quantum ice fractalling outward from their engines, from the circuits of their dashboards. The ice has burst from their chassis, creating random new configurations of ice, technology, and anatomy.

There was no warning. In one moment the world changed: this is the ice age.

On our bicycles, Mark and I zigzag through the permanently stalled traffic. I try not to stare at the damaged bodies. But Mark is too engrossed to notice my queasiness. Too giddy. Goofy, even. For so many reasons, we were right to leave. Already, his face is brighter.

"Hey, Martha . . . Did you see that couple in the blue SUV?"

I wish I hadn't: ice snaked around their heads, crushing

251

them together.

"Did you see—"

No, I didn't see. I don't look. At least I try not to. Mark copes in his own way; I can't fault him for doing it differently. He never told me how he lost his parents, and I never told him how I lost mine. I should be numb to such sights by now. In the city, they'd become part of the landscape; we'd ignored them. We'd been too cold to notice. Too cold to care. Barely out of the city, and already we're both thawing—at least a little.

I can't bring myself to tell him to stop. So I just pedal faster. I race off the Jacques Cartier Bridge onto the highway, where the number of cars on the road decreases with distance, leaving Montreal behind, heading for . . .

. . . For a new world? Maybe. A different world, at least. I just want us to belong somewhere.

People say the whole planet is like this now. But how can they be sure? Nothing works anymore. No television, no telephones, no computers, no radios. There's no way to communicate.

But they must be right. If the rest of the world were still intact, someone would have rescued us by now. The Army. The United States. Someone. Anyone.

"Martha!"

I look back, and Mark is pedalling hard to catch up to me.

I love how the wind lifts his long, dark hair. His smile is like a little boy's. Already, I've forgiven him for being so morbid, for being so wrapped up in his grotesque passion that he couldn't notice my distress.

Since I've known him, Mark has always protected me. Now he's relaxing about that. I like him even more this way.

He catches up to me, and we stop. We gaze at the transmuted cityscape we are leaving behind.

The sunlight's reflection almost blinds me; ice blankets the Island of Montreal. The skyscrapers of the financial district have been transformed into macabre, twisted spires. The tall downtown hotels bulge with ice—the tumorous limbs of a tentacled leviathan. Like a bed of gems, the city catches the sunlight and glows. Even the heat generated by all this light cannot dispel the cold. The air carries an autumn chill, even though it's mid-July. The ice radiates cold. It never melts; it's so hard it can't even break.

The Quantum Cross, the icon of the city's new order, rests atop Mount Royal.

I close my eyes, not yet ready to cry. Eager to forget. But the memories come anyway.

All I did was shut my eyes, and the world took on a new shape.

Sunday afternoon: my sister in the upstairs bathroom, obsessing over her looks; my parents driving out to the airport to meet Grandma. Me: by the living room window, reading a book, curled up in the coziest armchair. I can't remember which book.

Here's what I remember: the sky was radiantly blue, and the sunlight hit the window with a harsh brightness. I had a slight headache. From reading, from the light.

Music: a trance/jungle mix spun in the CD player.

I closed my eyes. The music stopped abruptly. I heard a weird crunching sound. A cool wave washed over me. My eyes snapped open. The television looked like a cubist mobile of the Milky Way. In place of the stereo, a crystal statue of a lizard demon crowned with looping horns. The lamps were now surrealist bouquets. Pearly spikes punched through the walls, especially near electrical outlets and lightswitches.

In the distance, screams rose against the background of cold silence.

I shivered.

My sister, Jocelyne, would never meet her boyfriend again. In the upstairs bathroom I found her skull, neck, and chest skewered by the ice sprouting from her hairdryer.

I hurried outside, onto streets lined with transformed buildings, arrayed with wrecked, deformed vehicles. Wires barbed with ice dangled from poles and walls, lay splattered all over. An instant alien landscape transposed onto a familiar urban grid.

I ran. It was all I could do. I ran, trying to escape the affected zone. I ran. And ran.

Until I stumbled on my parents' car. They were smeared on the seat leather, pulverized by the ice.

I looked around. I'd reached the expressway. As far as I could see, there was evidence of the transformation. For the first time I noticed the new shape of the giant electric cross atop Mount Royal: a violent explosion frozen midblast. Towering over the city, the metamorphosed cross kept a vigil over this new world, claiming dominion.

Since that first day, I hadn't ventured outside. How long ago had that been? I was almost out of food. I awoke sporadically. Sometimes I snacked on stale crackers. I'd exhausted the canned goods. Days ago? Weeks?

In this new ice age, the ceaseless hum of automobile traffic had finally been quieted. The sound of airplanes no longer wafted down from above.

The city was silent. Cold and silent. I felt that silence in the hollow of my bones. The cold had seeped into me, had hardened my insides, had slowed the beat of my heart.

I stared out the window at the unchanging landscape and fell asleep again, to dreams of silent jets falling from the sky.

Even in my dreams, I heard him. Yet, I stayed asleep. The sounds of him taking and releasing his breath replaced the silenced engines.

Eventually, I woke, his presence gradually imprinting itself on me. And then I saw him: sitting on the edge of my bed.

He said, "Hi," neither smiling nor frowning. Waiting.

He had long black hair, and he was maybe a year or two older—almost a man. But he had the face of a little boy, and dark eyes so big that I saw deep into him, saw how he'd been hurt by the coldness of the world. Although I had never met him before, I knew him. In that moment I knew him.

"My name is Mark," he said; louder than a whisper, but without inflection.

I rested my head on his thigh. The touch of his callused fingertips against my scalp shot sparks of warmth through my body, began thawing the cold that had settled within me. I filled my lungs with air. The smell of his sweat eased the flow of my blood. I let go of my breath and moaned drowsily. I fell asleep again. No more falling jets. Finally, I rested.

"Quantum ice. Call it *quantum ice*." Daniel coined the term. The expression stuck. We heard it whispered everywhere by Montrealers who roamed their transfigured city like zombies.

Daniel was Mark's brother, but they were so different. Mark was tall and calm. Handsome. Daniel was short and nervous. Funny looking, in a bad way. And loud. Always chattering, listening to himself rhapsodize. His eyes were wild, always darting here and there, unable to focus on anything, or on anyone.

We saw Daniel infrequently. Usually when he wanted to bum food off his brother. Mark wanted him to stay with us, but, to my relief, Daniel resisted the idea. He'd disappear for days, waiting for Mark to fall asleep before he wandered off.

Daniel had his theory about the ice age. A bomb, he thought. A quantum bomb. The project of the rogue R&D department of some corporate weapons manufacturer. He claimed his blogging community used to keep track of things like that. He said reality—physics—had been changed at a fundamental level. Old technologies no longer worked. We needed a new scientific paradigm. Other things might have changed. Our bodies might not work quite the same way anymore. Nature might have changed. The food chain. The air. Gravity.

Daniel was a bit younger than I was; he certainly couldn't have been more than fifteen. He looked like the type who, before the ice age, got beat up on his way home from school. But the ice age had changed him; it had changed everyone. Daniel spoke with the intensity of the insane. A prophet desperate to convert his audience.

He was full of shit. Daniel was as ignorant as the rest of us. Nobody could know the truth. Maybe the ice had really been caused by aliens, or by magic, or . . . Maybe God had sneezed, or something. Probably, yes, it had been a bomb. Did it really matter? We couldn't bring back the dead. Besides, there was no proof anything beyond electrical technology had been affected. Fractals of quantum ice had erupted from the cores of our machines, from the wires that carried electricity, from the circuits and engines that fed on electric power. It had taken at most a few seconds between when everything stopped working and when the quantum ice appeared and expanded.

The state of the world: this strange new ice age.

Society had broken down. No social workers swooping down on orphaned kids. We had to take care of ourselves now. No more school. I didn't miss it. I didn't miss the jerks staring at my suddenly developed breasts. I didn't miss the other girls thinking I was too bookish and nerdy to be friends with.

Some fears make you flee, others make you stay. Mark said hundreds of thousands of people had already left the city. Many more must have died. At least a million people, we estimated. In hospitals. In cars. In elevators. On escalators. In front of computers. Using appliances. Snapping photos. Shooting videos. Taking food out of the fridge. Carrying a phone in your pocket meant ice bored into your pelvis. The technology that triggered the ice was everywhere.

The corpses, too, were everywhere. The city should have reeked of rot and decay, but the ice preserved what it touched. I ignored the dead. Every day, no matter where we went, Mark and I saw the bodies claimed by the ice, but we never mentioned them.

There were still thousands of survivors who had stayed behind. They wandered the streets, lost, alone, barely aware of each other. The cold seeped into everyone.

Mark kept me warm, but I still hadn't thawed completely. I hadn't even cried yet. The placid coolness of the ice age, that utter absence of emotion, was almost comforting.

Together, Mark and I fought off the encroaching cold.

We played hide-and-seek in deserted malls. The electronics shops were frozen supernovas.

We explored the metro tunnels. The flames of hand-held torches, reflected on blooms of quantum ice, lit our way.

We walked on rooftops, holding hands, the ice-encrusted city spread below us.

At night, Mark spooned me. We went to bed with our clothes

on. I took his hand and slipped it under my shirt, holding it tight against my stomach. He nuzzled my hair.

He always woke before me. Always came back with scavenged food.

One day, maybe we'd kiss.

Daniel acquired followers. He changed his name to Danny Quantum and started believing his own hype. It was creepy, the way these lost people gravitated toward him—obeyed him, even. Orphaned kids. Businessmen in suits that had known better days. Middle-aged women with hungry, desperate looks. Cybergeeks bereft of their only lifeline.

Daniel and his followers gathered in the heart of the city, on Mount Royal, below that monstrous thing that had once been a cross. Daniel turned it into the symbol of his new religion. He didn't use the word *religion*, but that's what it was.

Mark brought me to Daniel's sermons. Daniel didn't use the word *sermon*, but that's what they were.

Feel-good catchphrases tinted with Nietzsche. New Age gobbledygook rationalized with scientific jargon. Cyberpunk animism. Catholic pomp sprinkled with evangelical alarmism. Eroticized psychobabble. Robert Bly mixed with Timothy Leary.

We'd climbed up some trees on the outer edge of the area where Danny Quantum's rapt disciples sat and listened to the sermon. We heard every word. Daniel knew how to pitch his voice. He was good at this. Too good.

I said, "Don't tell me you believe any of this nonsense."

For the first time, it occurred to me that maybe I couldn't trust Mark. The cold seized my heart.

He said, "Of course not. But somebody has to keep an eye on Daniel. Who else is going to look out for him? Especially now." Mark looked away as he spoke.

As far as Mark was aware, his brother was the only person he knew from before who'd survived the ice age—or who hadn't left without a word in the initial panic. That Daniel was scary, that he was dangerous, Mark wasn't ready to acknowledge.

A fractallized airplane blocked the intersection of St-Laurent and Ste-Catherine, its tail propped up by the ice-encrusted building on the corner, the tip of its nose run through the storefront window of a store the ice had altered beyond recognition. Even the force of a plane crash couldn't shatter the quantum ice. Briefly, I wondered if it might have been Grandma's plane.

Someone had painted a likeness of the transmogrified cross on the hull, with the words *The Quantum Cross of the Ice Age* below it. That day, everywhere we went, we noticed fresh graffiti of the Quantum Cross, on the asphalt of the streets, on store windows, on sidewalks, on brick walls, on concrete blocks.

The next day, Mark and I bicycled out to the airport and stared at the planes: massive dinosaurs with limbs of ice, gore, metal, and plastic.

Before going home—neither my old home nor Mark's, but an abandoned townhouse near McGill University whose windows faced away from Mount Royal—Mark wanted to check in on his little brother. These days, Daniel never left the mountain. His acolytes brought food to him. Brought themselves to him.

I complained. "I'm too tired to bicycle all the way up there." More truthfully, I was increasingly queasy around Daniel and his sycophants, and I was eager to collapse in Mark's arms, even though the sun hadn't set.

He insisted.

So we wound our way up the sinuous gravel path, occasionally encountering Daniel's followers. Despite the cold, they wore white T-shirts—no coats, no jackets, no sweaters. On the shirts, in red, were crude drawings in thick dripping lines: bloody effigies of the Quantum Cross.

When we reached the cross itself, where Daniel's congregation assembled, I noticed that they were all dressed this way, no longer individuals but a hive functioning with a single mind. Danny Quantum's.

First I heard the singing. Mark had just beaten me at croquet for the third game in a row. I looked around, and then I spotted them: to the south of the croquet park, twenty or so people walking down the Jacques Cartier Bridge into Montreal.

One of them pointed at us, and the group headed our way. They waved and kept on singing. I thought I recognized the song. Something from the 1960s. The kind of stuff my parents listened to.

Mark waved back. He said, "Hold on to your mallet. If things get rough, swing for the head and knee them in the crotch."

They seemed harmless. Approximately as many men as women. Long hair. Handmade clothes. Artsy-crafty jewellery. A bunch of latter-day hippies. The song wound down when they reached the edge of the park. I noticed a few of them looked more like bikers. I tightened my grip.

Only one of them came up to us. The one who looked more *Saturday Night Fever* than *Hair*.

He said, "Peace."

Mark said, "Hi. Where are you folks from?"

"I'm from New York City. But we're from all over. Vermont. Ottawa. Maine. Sherbrooke."

Mark asked, "So, it's like this everywhere?"

"It's like this everywhere we've been. The whole world has changed. So many tragic deaths." But he made it sound almost cheerful, like a TV ad.

Mark grunted. Something about Saturday Night Fever— his calculating eyes, his used-car salesman voice—made me distrust him immediately.

"Are you two youngsters alone? It's safer to stay in a large group. We're gathering people to form a commune. To survive in this new age. To repopulate. We need children. Strong, healthy children."

His eyes appraised me, lingering on my hips. I tensed my arms, ready to swing. Mark shifted, his body shielding me from Saturday Night Fever's gaze.

"Well, I wish you folks the best. It sounds like a great project."

"You and your friend should join us. We'd be happy

to welcome you." He addressed Mark, but his eyes kept straying to my body.

"Thanks, but we're good here. This is home."

Three of the men in the group were big. Wrestler big. No way Mark and I could stop them if they decided to add me to their baby factory by force.

"Are you sure?"

"Yeah. Anyway, we should be on our way. Good luck." Mark took my hand, and we walked away. We held on to our mallets.

Mark slept. He didn't know, but I'd stayed awake through the previous two nights.

His mouth was slightly open, and he was almost snoring. I loved all of his sounds, even the silly ones. I traced his lips with my index finger; it didn't rouse him, but he moaned. It was a delicious noise.

I stared at him all night, scrutinizing every detail of him.

Dawn broke. As Mark stirred, I pretended to sleep.

The night Danny Quantum and his followers started sacrificing cats and dogs, I told Mark, "We have to leave."

I was bundled under three layers of sweaters, but the cold still bit. Even the heat from the fires around the Quantum Cross couldn't keep me warm. I was tempted to lean into Mark, for warmth, for comfort, but I needed to talk to him, and for that I had to stay focused.

"You tired?"

"No. I mean, go away. Off the island. Leave all this behind. Find somewhere else to live. Somewhere far. Somewhere safer."

I wanted him to say, *Yes, I'll go anywhere with you.*

He said, "Who'll protect Daniel? If I go, he'll just get worse. He'll be lost forever."

"Then talk to him. Make him stop this before . . ."

"It's not that easy. Not that simple. He doesn't hear what he doesn't want to. This is his way of coping. We've all lost too much."

"You know where this is heading. Soon, it'll be people being shishkebabed to satisfy Danny Quantum's megalomania. To feed the hungry bellies of his flock."

I didn't look at Mark. I didn't want his dark eyes to sway me. I stared at the fires burning at the foot of the Quantum Cross. I looked at Daniel, prancing and shouting. Like the maniac that he was.

"I'm leaving tomorrow morning. Getting away from Daniel. Far away. Find somewhere to grow food. Somewhere with fresh water. Head south, maybe."

Could I leave without Mark? I wanted to kiss him. Would I ever? Even after all we'd shared, the cold still held our hearts in its grip.

"Don't, Martha. Don't make me choose." He turned his face away from mine and stared at his brother in the distance. When he continued, his voice was firm—firm enough to sting. "Besides, we've always lived in the city. What do you know about farming, or even about gathering food in the wild?"

"We can learn how to survive." Despite myself, doubt had crept into my voice.

Was I willing to stay and let this drama play out, despite its inevitable horrors? Wherever I would end up away from here, there might be other Saturday Night Fevers or Danny Quantums. Or maybe even worse.

One of Danny's people handed Mark a wooden stick. There was a roasted, skewered cat on it.

I said, "Are you going to eat that?"

He said, "I'll go with you. Anywhere."

The wind on my face, the smell of grass and trees tickling my nose, I race down the deserted road.

Mark is with me. Laughing. I laugh, too.

In the fields there are cows. Horses. Dogs. Sometimes people.

Some of them wave at us, smiling. Some of them shoot at us, warning us away.

We're not ready to stop yet.

AFTERWORD:
BEHIND THE SCENES WITH CLAUDE LALUMIÈRE

1. **The Object of Worship**

"The Object of Worship" is both a tribute and a response to Rachel Pollack's magnum opus, *Unquenchable Fire*, one of my favourite novels. *Unquenchable Fire* had a tremendous impact on my imagination. Its use of primal mythic rituals in an urban setting and its particular manner of presenting the strange as commonplace spoke to me quite profoundly and proved to be very influential on my own writing. As a work of art it has never stopped growing within me since I first read it in 1989. The way *Unquenchable Fire* deals with pregnancy has always disturbed me—and not necessarily in a good way. Thus, this story—working out both the literary influence of and my queasiness with Pollack's complex and alluring masterpiece.

2. The Ethical Treatment of Meat

It's been said by others that writing fiction is an act of creative misreading. Certainly, that's true of "The Object of Worship" as a misreading of *Unquenchable Fire*. In fact, many of my stories are partly a result of working through intentional misreadings. But no story of mine is more directly the result of a misreading than "The Ethical Treatment of Meat." I began to glimpse this story when an ambiguity in the first paragraph of an early draft of Dora Knez's zombie story "The Dead Park" led me to misunderstand which characters were zombies and which were alive. My confusion caused me to imagine an entirely different story than the one Dora hoped to convey. Soon after, I saw a call for submissions for *The Book of More Flesh*, asking for unusual zombie stories. Synchronicity is hard to resist: my zombie idea, already unusual to start with, continued to evolve, taking on elements from 1960s monster sitcoms *The Munsters* and *The Addams Family* and from Kyle Baker's 1992 comics story "Lester Fenton and the Walking Dead," until it became a story of its own—and even more unusual. My story was indeed published in *The Book of More Flesh* in 2002, while the final version of Dora Knez's "The Dead Park" appeared in *Island Dreams: Montreal Writers of the Fantastic*, which I edited the following year. "The Ethical Treatment of Meat" has been taught in a number of high schools around Montreal. It's always a blast to meet the students and discuss with them the various issues and themes raised in this story.

3. **Hochelaga and Sons**

I love superhero comics, as "Hochelaga and Sons" makes blatantly obvious. A lifetime of superhero comics reading fed into this story, but three sources are clearly foremost. First, Bernie Mireault's *The Jam*—about an ordinary Montrealer who decides to put on a modified gym suit and pretend to be a superhero while hanging out on rooftops—is one of my favourite comics of the 1980s, and the spirit of that series is all over this story, especially in regards to the personality of the father. Second, both the narrative point-of-view and the manner in which I play with superhero archetypes evoke Kurt Busiek's *Astro City*. And, third, there's Jack Kirby, the King of Comics and one of the greatest cartoonists of all time. Probably, he's an influence in some way or other on most of what I write. But in this case I can trace back a direct influence, from a 1963 story: "The Hate-Monger!" (*Fantastic Four* #21)—one of the many times that Kirby explored the idea of fascism as the ultimate form of human evil and also where we can find the seeds of later, more ambitious explorations of that idea, for example in *New Gods* and *OMAC: One Man Army Corps*. But more on Kirby below, in the note on "Destroyer of Worlds."

4. **The Sea, at Bari**

Ever since early childhood, I have had a deeply mythic and emotional connection to large bodies of water. During a

2006 trip to Europe, I found myself in Bari, Italy, barefoot in the waters of the Adriatic Sea. With the smells, sounds, and sights of the sea engulfing me, this story came to me, unbidden. I composed most of it in my head right there. That evening, I was boarding a boat for Greece. The final pieces came into place while I was standing on deck as the boat ventured out into the darkness of the nighttime sea. In my cabin, I furiously typed "The Sea, at Bari" on my laptop.

5. **The Darkness at the Heart of the World**

My Lost Pages sequence—a series of six urban fantasies focusing on a bookshop that serves as a nexus between realities—has all kinds of mythological shenanigans going on in the background. I wanted to explore that mythological backstory, but freed from the concerns, characters, themes, and overarching plot of the Lost Pages series itself. Thus this story, in which I pay tribute to both the mythological fantasies of Lord Dunsany and the Flat Earth stories of Tanith Lee.

6. **Spiderkid**

I'd just finished writing the first (of many!) drafts of the long-gestating "Destroyer of Worlds" (see below), and I was eager to tackle something else—something shorter and less difficult to wrestle into shape. "Destroyer of Worlds" owes a huge debt to Jack Kirby, but there was an outtake where I'd had some fun pastiching the work of Kirby's 1960s Marvel Comics colleague Steve Ditko, co-creator of Spider-

Man and Doctor Strange. Out of that unused snippet grew "Spiderkid"—a loving tribute to the work of Steve Ditko, although I'm sure the ultra-conservative Ditko would disapprove of many elements in this story. Another irony is that the snippet in question did not survive the final edit of "Spiderkid" either. I still have it lurking in my files . . . I'm hoping something else will come out of it at some point.

7. **Njàbò**

The lives and plight of nonhuman animals in our human-dominated world has been a concern of mine since early childhood. One of the most fascinating books I've read on the subject of the clash between human and animal societies is *Natural Enemies: People-Wildlife Conflicts in Anthropological Perspective*, edited by John Knight. It's there that I found the inspiration for "Njàbò": namely, in Alex Köhler's essay "Half-Man, Half-Elephant: Shapeshifting among the Baka of Congo." I should state that, for dramatic purposes, I took many liberties with Baka lore, and any discrepancies with reality should in no way be attributed to Köhler but entirely to me.

8. **A Place Where Nothing Ever Happens**

I'd been reading quite a lot of Paul Di Filippo's short fiction, including his many goofball romantic comedies in sciencefictional settings, typically starring hapless and clueless male leads opposite utterly charming female co-stars. So I thought I'd try my hand at one such story (albeit in a more fantastical mode), at the same time turning on its head the Talking Heads' notion that "Heaven is a place where nothing ever happens."

9. **A Visit to the Optometrist**
The Fespers—the neighbours from "The Ethical Treatment of Meat"—were not part of my original conception of that earlier story. They emerged during the writing and took on a life of their own. By the end of that story I loved them so much that I knew I would one day write another zombie story with them as the focus. I didn't want to force it, so I filed that notion away in the back of my mind until the right story presented itself. A few years later, "A Visit to the Optometrist" just popped out of my subconscious with no warning.

10. **Roman Predator's Chimeric Odyssey**
"Roman Predator's Chimeric Odyssey" is an example of a story eventually emerging from a long-gestating opening scene. I blundered through more than a few false starts, but I kept junking everything except for that opening and then letting it sit for a few months before tackling it again. Eventually, something stuck, and this story took shape. The inspiration for "Roman Predator's Chimeric Odyssey" came from several totally unrelated short stories by Robert Reed, but heavily filtered through my own preoccupations and sensibilities.

11. **Destroyer of Worlds**
Any reader of Jack Kirby's comics will easily find echoes

here from, especially, *Fantastic Four* and *New Gods*. And, of course, Jake Kurtz, as an aspect of Brahma the Creator, is explicitly intended to be a doppelganger of Kirby himself, one of the people whose oeuvre has had the most impact on me. I just about worship Kirby's work—it was inevitable that I would dip into that well for inspiration. The first thing that came to me was the opening scene—the original version of which predates by more than a decade the period I started writing seriously. Talk about a long gestation period! And that had nothing to do with Kirby at first; rather, it was a response to (i.e., a creative misreading of) the framing sequence in Theodore Sturgeon's "A Saucer of Loneliness." Over the years, I became increasingly obsessed with that scene, rewriting it over and over again into various stories that failed to go anywhere. Finally one of my many attempts bore fruit, and "Destroyer of Worlds" poured out of me. At one point it was twice as long as it ended up being; it went through more revisions than anything else I've written. Other stuff got thrown into the final mix, most notably Roger Zelazny (especially his early mythology/SF hybrids) and the 1960s British TV series *The Champions*.

12. **This Is the Ice Age**

Julie Czerneda and Genevieve Kierans invited me to contribute to their anthology *Mythspring: From the Lyrics & Legends of Canada*. The idea was to take inspiration from a Canadian song or legend and forge an entirely new story. Instead of the expected folkloric sources, I opted for Canadian New Wave band Martha & the Muffins and their haunting and hypnotic sciencefictional song "This Is the Ice Age." In fact, many songs, and even the cover art and design, from the album of the same name fed into the tapestry of the story. Since I was clearly crafting a disaster story, I decided to also pay homage to the greatest disaster novelist of the twentieth century, and my favourite writer, J.G. Ballard, as Ballard readers will easily notice. One of the coolest things that happened as a result of this story was that I got to meet Mark Gane and Martha Johnson, the musicians at the heart of Martha & the Muffins.

ACKNOWLEDGEMENTS

"The Object of Worship" first appeared in *Tesseracts Eleven* (Edge Publishing 2007), edited by Cory Doctorow & Holly Phillips.

"The Ethical Treatment of Meat" first appeared in *The Book of More Flesh* (Eden Studios 2002), edited by James Lowder.

"Hochelaga and Sons" first appeared in *Electric Velocipede* #13 (Fall 2007).

"The Sea, at Bari" first appeared in *On Spec* #72 (Spring 2008).

"The Darkness at the Heart of the World" is previously unpublished.

"Spiderkid" first appeared in *Reflection's Edge* #22 (February 2007).

"Njàbò" previously appeared in *On Spec* #54 (Fall 2003), Kenoma (December 2004), and *Expanded Horizons* #1 (October 2008).

"A Place Where Nothing Ever Happens" first appeared in *Interzone* #182 (November 2002).

"A Visit to the Optometrist" previously appeared in *SDO Fantasy* (October 2004) and in *The Best of SDO* (Perplexed Puffin Press 2005), edited by Mark Anthony Brennan & David Bowlin.

"Roman Predator's Chimeric Odyssey" is previously unpublished.

"Destroyer of Worlds" first appeared in *Electric Velocipede* #15/16 (Winter 2008).

"This Is the Ice Age" previously appeared in *Mythspring* (Red Deer Press 2006), edited by Julie Czerneda & Genevieve Kierans, and in *Year's Best SF 12* (Eos 2007), edited by David Hartwell & Kathryn Cramer.

ABOUT THE AUTHOR

CLAUDE LALUMIÈRE

Claude Lalumière (lostpages.net) is the editor of eight anthologies, including *Island Dreams: Montreal Writers of the Fantastic* and the Aurora Award-nominated *Tesseracts Twelve: New Novellas of Canadian Fantastic Fiction*. He writes the Fantastic Fiction column for *The Montreal Gazette*. Claude is the co-creator, with artist Rupert Bottenberg, of Lost Myths (lostmyths.net).